LEONARD'S
GOLDEN TOUCH

"[The book has] Leonard's fish-hard
way with words,
dialogue that seems to come straight
from a hidden tape-recorder,
sharply chiseled characters,
and a style that compels readers
to keep turning the pages."
Philadelphia Inquirer

"Infinitely touching and funny"
San Francisco Chronicle

"His most appealing novel . . .
a magic 'Touch.'"
Detroit News

"The gritty, street-smart dialogue,
Leonard's trademark,
is as good as it gets."
Newsday

"Will almost certainly
be another of Leonard's big hits"
Publishers Weekly

"Thoroughly entertaining"
Chicago Tribune

TOUCH

Elmore Leonard

AVON BOOKS ⬢ NEW YORK

AVON BOOKS
A division of
The Hearst Corporation
105 Madison Avenue
New York, New York 10016

Published in hardcover by Arbor House/William Morrow and Company,
Inc.; for information address Permissions Department, William Morrow
and Company, Inc., 105 Madison Avenue, New York, New York 10016.

First Avon Books Printing: September 1988

AVON TRADEMARK REG. U.S. PAT. OFF. AND IN OTHER COUNTRIES, MARCA
REGISTRADA, HECHO EN U.S.A.

Printed in the U.S.A.

K-R 10 9 8 7 6 5 4 3 2 1

FOR JOHN CARLSON

TOUCH

1

Frank Sinatra, Jr., was saying, "I don't have to take this," getting up out of the guest chair, walking out. Howard Hart was grinning at him with his capped teeth.

Virginia was saying, "What's Frank Sinatra, Jr., doing? What's Howard Hart doing?"

Elwin sidearmed an empty Early Times bottle at the TV set, shattering the sixteen-inch screen, wiping out Howard Hart's grin and Frank Sinatra, Jr., going out the door. Elwin took down the presidential plates from the rail over the couch—Eisenhower, Kennedy, Lyndon Johnson and Lady Bird, Richard Nixon and Gerald Ford, all the portraits done in color—and sailed the plates one at a time at the piano, trying to skim off the silver-framed photograph of Virginia seated at the console of the Mighty Hammond organ. He missed five out of five but destroyed each of the plates against the wall back of the piano. The Early Times bottle was still good, so he smashed the photograph with that, looked around for something else, and threw the bottle end over end, like a tomahawk, exploding the big picture window for the high ultimate in glass-shattering noise.

Then he grabbed Virginia, the real Virginia—thirty pounds heavier than the smiling organist in the photograph—and as she pushed and clawed at him, trying to get loose, he threw a wild punch that grazed her head and set her screaming. Finally he was able to connect with a good one, belting her square in the face, grazing that long, skinny nose, hitting her hard enough that he hurt his hand and had to go out in the kitchen and run water on it.

When Bill Hill arrived Elwin let him in and went back through the living room to the kitchen, saying only, "She called you, huh? When she do that?" Elwin didn't care if he got an answer. He reached up to a top cupboard shelf and pulled a fifth of Jim Beam from behind the garden-fresh canned peas and cream-style corn.

Bill Hill had on his good light blue summer suit and a burgundy sport shirt with the collar open to show the heavy gold chain and medallion that was inscribed *Thank you, Jesus*. He had his dark hair swirled down over his forehead and sprayed hard, ready to go out for the evening, almost out the door when Virginia called. She was on the sofa now sobbing into a little satin pillow. He bent over her and said, "Here, let me see," gently taking the pillow from her face. The dark hollows of her eyes were wet, her rouge smeared and streaked, one side of her face swollen as though she had an abscessed tooth. The skin was scraped, beginning to show a bruise, but it wasn't cut or bleeding.

"What'd he hit you with, his fist?"

Virginia nodded, trying to raise the pillow again to her face. The satin material was probably cool and it was a place to hide. Bill Hill held onto the pillow, wanting her to look up at him.

"How long's he been drinking? All day?"

"All day, all yesterday." Virginia was trying to talk without moving her mouth. "I called the Center, it was about an hour ago, but nobody came. So I called you."

"I'll get you a wet cloth, okay? You're gonna be all right, Ginny. Then I'll have a talk with him."

"He never was this bad, all the other times."

"Well, they get worse," Bill Hill said, "from what I understand."

It was hot and close in the house and smelled of stale cigarette smoke, though the attic fan was going, sounding like an airplane in the upstairs hall. Elwin had a hip pressed against the sink, using a butcher knife on the Jim Beam seal. His shirt was messy, sweat-stained. His old-timey-looking slick hair hung down on both sides of his face from the part that showed white scalp and was always straight as a ruler no matter how drunk he got.

Bill Hill said, "You're a beauty. You know it?"

"I'm glad you come over to give me some of your mouth," Elwin said. "That goddamn woman, I got her shut up for a while, now I got you starting on me. Why don't you just get the hell out of here. I didn't invite you, I know goddamn well." He got the top off and poured half a jelly glass full of Jim Beam and added a splash of Seven-Up from a bottle on the counter. The sink was full of dishes and an empty milk carton. Elwin said, "You want a drink, help yourself."

"I want to know what's wrong with you," Bill Hill said, "beating up on Ginny like that. You realize what you did?"

"I realize I shut her goddamn mouth. I warned her," Elwin said. "I told her, Jesus, shut your mouth for a while, give us some peace. She kept right on." Elwin's voice rose, mimicking, as he said, " 'What're you doing, you drinking again? Getting drunk, aren't you, sucking on your whiskey bottle.' I said I'm having a couple for my goddamn nerves to lie still."

"For a couple of days," Bill Hill said. "But I guess you know what you're doing, don't you?"

"I got her shut up," Elwin said. "How many times I said, *Shut up!* She kept right on, yak yak yak, her mouth working like it'd never stop. Yak yak yak yak, Jesus."

"Well, you stopped her," Bill Hill said. "You gonna take her to the hospital or you want me to?"

"Hospital, shit, there's nothing wrong with her. I give her a little shove."

"Well, what if she's got a concussion of the brain," Bill Hill said, "you ever consider that? You want to come out and take a look at your wife you got up the courage to belt in the face with your fist. You're pretty brave, Elwin, I'll say that for you."

"You won't be saying nothing you keep it up," Elwin said, "you'll be spitting your teeth."

"Okay, you're tough, Elwin, and I'm scared," Bill Hill said. "But you want to talk to me a minute? Try to explain to me what happened? See, maybe I'm dumb or something. I don't understand a man taking a punch at his wife and tearing up his living room. You remember doing all that?"

"I'll tell you what the hell happened," Elwin said, "feeling that goddamn woman watching me, following me around—"

"Now wait a minute," Bill Hill said, "you're watching yourself is who's watching anybody and you know it. That's called having a guilty conscience. You hide those bottles you're hiding them from yourself."

"Bull*shit*, you think she can't find them? She *feels* all over this goddamn house, buddy, and she finds them."

"All right, you know what I'm saying," Bill Hill said. "You try not to drink for a while, you go to meetings and you get along pretty good, don't you? Then you give in, and you know what happens every time. You smash up your car. You run clear through your garage wall out the back. You start punching people—hitting guys, that's bad enough. Now you're punching your poor, defenseless wife—"

"Poor, defenseless shit—"

"Listen to me, all right? Will you just listen a minute?"

"Poor, defenseless mouth going all day long."

"Elwin, what happens every time? You smash something, don't you? Or some*body*. And you end up in jail or back in the Rehabilitation Center. Is that the way you want to live?"

"I got a good idea," Elwin said.

"Okay, tell me what it is." Bill Hill looked up at him calmly. Elwin was several inches taller than Bill Hill's five nine and with big, hard bones and big, gnarled hands that looked like tree roots, working man's hands.

"Why don't you get out of here," Elwin said, "before I heave you right through the screen door. You believe I can't do it?"

"No, I believe you can," Bill Hill said, "but instead of that, why don't we see if we can get Ginny fixed up a little. What do you say?" He took a dish towel that was fairly clean and ran it under cold water and wrung it out and folded the cloth, trying not to get his suit wet or mussed up, while Elwin told him again how the woman never shut up from the time she got out of bed in the morning to the time she crawled back in at night and lay there bitching in the dark, all day while he'd be trying to do some work around the house or else reading the want ads in both Detroit papers and the *Oakland County Press,* but was there any construction work? Shit no, cause they was letting the niggers in the union and giving them all the jobs. Then Elwin dropped his drink on the floor and had to make a new one.

Virginia looked worn out and in pain, a poor, battered wife of a laid-off construction worker. Bill Hill got her stretched out on the sofa with a pile of little pillows beneath her head. She'd moan something as he wiped off her face. He'd say, "What?" Then finally realized she was just making sounds, down in there being miserable.

He went out to the kitchen to rinse the dishcloth and told Elwin why didn't he, instead of standing there getting shit-face drunker than he already was, why didn't he straighten up the mess in the kitchen.

That was a big mistake.

Elwin said okay, he'd straighten up the mess, and began taking dishes out of the sink and dropping them on the floor, saying to Bill Hill how's that? Was that straight enough for him?

Bill Hill went back to the living room and laid the cool, damp cloth over Virginia's eyes, hearing Elwin dropping dishes and the dishes smashing on the floor. Bill Hill had a date and was going to a disco. He was thinking, Shit, he might never make it and the girl would get mad and pout sitting home with her hair done and her perfume on.

The young guy in jeans and a striped T-shirt and sneakers opened the aluminum screen door and walked in. Standing there with his fingers wedged in his pants pockets, he said, "This is the Worrels', isn't it?" Then seemed to smile a little as he saw Elwin in the kitchen dropping dishes. He said, "Yeah, I think I recognize somebody." He looked at Bill Hill and then at Virginia on the sofa. "What happened?"

"You a friend of the Worrels?" Bill Hill was guarded. He didn't know who this young guy was. But maybe the young guy had seen this show before and that's why he wasn't surprised or seemed disturbed.

"I know Elwin a little bit," the young guy said. "From when he was at Sacred Heart. They just called me to see if I could stop by, maybe talk to him. I'm Juvenal." He was looking at Virginia again, frowning a little now. "Is she all right?"

"Oh, you're from the Center," Bill Hill said. "Good. You're just the man we need." Though the young guy—

Juvenal?—didn't look anything like an AA house caller, a man who'd been there and back and could understand what the drunk was going through. This one looked like a college student dressed for a picnic. No, older than that. But skinny, immature-looking, light-brown hair down over his forehead, cut sort of short. He looked like a nice, well-behaved boy that mothers of young girls would love to see come to the house.

"You said your name's . . . Juvenal?"

"That's right." The young guy raised his voice and said, "Elwin, what're you doing?"

"He's breaking dishes," Bill Hill said. What was the young guy smiling about? No, he wasn't smiling. But he seemed to be smiling, his expression relaxed, as though nothing at all was on his mind. He certainly didn't look like a drunk. He hardly looked old enough even to get a drink. Bill Hill bet, though, he was about thirty.

Elwin was hollering now, swearing goddamn it he'd get the goddamn kitchen straightened, reaching up to the cupboard to get more dishes. The young guy, Juvenal, walked past Bill Hill out of the living room to the kitchen. Bill Hill heard Elwin's voice again, then nothing. Silence. He could see the young guy saying something to Elwin, but couldn't hear him. Elwin seemed to be listening, nodding, the young guy talking with his hands in his pockets.

Bill Hill said, "Christ Almighty."

Maybe the young guy did know what he was doing. Bill Hill walked over to the kitchen doorway to see Elwin getting a broom and dustpan out of the closet. The young guy, Juvenal, was picking up Elwin's drink.

Now he'll pour it out, Bill Hill thought. Jesus, help us. And Elwin'll go berserk again.

But the young guy didn't pour it out. He took a good sip of the Jim Beam drink and put it down on the yellow tile counter again.

What the hell kind of an AA caller was he anyway? The young guy came toward Bill Hill but was looking past him into the living room.

"Is she all right?"

"I think so. He belted her a good one, but I don't believe he busted anything."

Now Elwin was leaning on his broom looking at Bill Hill. "All done," he said. "You gonna stand there with your finger up your ass or you gonna help me?"

Bill Hill said, tired, "Yeah, I'll help you." He started past the young guy.

"What's the matter with her?"

He was staring at Virginia on the sofa with the dishcloth folded over her eyes.

"He punched her in the face," Bill Hill said. "She's got a big bruise, so I put a cold cloth on it."

"No, I mean what else's wrong with her?" the young guy said. "Something is, isn't it?"

"Oh," Bill Hill said. "Well, yeah, she's blind."

"All her life?"

"Ever since I've known her." Bill Hill glanced over at the sofa, keeping his voice low. "Ginny got hit in the head in a car wreck about fifteen years ago. Yeah, in Sixty-two. It left her blind."

Juvenal moved past him.

Bill Hill watched him go over and look down at Virginia, his hands in his pockets, then the hands coming out of the pockets as he sat down on the edge of the sofa, his back to the kitchen. Bill Hill saw him raise the dishcloth from Virginia's eyes.

Elwin said, "You want to know something? Virginia's mother give us these dishes when we got married and all that time, Christ, twenty-one years, I hated those goddamn dishes. Got little rosebuds on 'em—"

Bill Hill turned to Elwin and took the dishpan from the table.

"—but I never said nothing. All that time, you'd get down through your mashed potatoes and wipe up your gravy? There'd be these little goddamn rosebuds looking at you. The only thing I said once, I said it looked like a goddamn little girl's tea set and Virginia got sore and started to cry. Shit, anything I didn't like, if I said it? She'd start to cry, like I was blaming her for it. I'd say goddamn it, what I think has got nothing to do with you, does it? She'll do it again. She'll reach up in the cupboard and say where's all my good dishes for heaven sake? And I'll tell her I got rid of those goddamn rosebud dishes *finally,* I finally got the nerve to get rid of them." Still rough talking, but his tone had changed, the meanness gone. Bill Hill noticed it.

He said, "Well, you might've bought some others first, since you're out of work and you got all this extra cash laying around."

"He come in here and says what're you doing. Juvie did," Elwin said. "I told him I always hated those goddamn rosebud dishes and I'm busting them. And he said, you know what he said? He said, 'I don't blame you.' "

Bill Hill wanted to ask about the young guy, who he was. Was he AA or not? Did he work at the Center in rehabilitation? If he did, how come he took a drink?

But Virginia began to call. She said, "Elwin?" In a sharp little surprised tone. She said, "Elwin, my God. Come here."

Both of them went into the living room, Elwin still holding the broom.

Virginia was sitting up, holding the dishcloth in her lap and turning her head carefully, as though she had a stiff neck, turning to the piano and then slowly turning her head toward the kitchen doorway. She looked different.

Elwin said, "Jesus, I cut her, didn't I?"

Bill Hill said, almost under his breath, "No, you

didn't. I'm sure you didn't.'' That was the whole thing, why he was more surprised than Elwin; because he had wiped off her face and looked at the bruise closely. Except for a scrape and the swelling there hadn't been a mark on her. But now there was a smear of blood on her face, over her forehead and cheeks. At least it looked like blood.

Bill Hill said, ''Ginny, you all right?''

Something scared him and kept him from moving.

He noticed now that the young guy, Juvenal, wasn't in the room. Though he might've gone up to the bathroom. Or he might've left. But that would be strange, coming here on a call and then leaving without saying anything.

Elwin said, ''Virginia, I got to tell you something.''

She said, ''Tell me.''

''Well, later on,'' Elwin said.

Bill Hill kept staring at her. What was it? She moved on the sofa, turning now to look directly at them. She looked worse than before. Battered, swollen, and now bloody. She seemed about to cry. But—what it was—she didn't seem miserable now. She was calm. She was *looking* at them out of dark shadows and her eyes were alive.

''What're you doing with a broom?'' Virginia said and seemed to smile, waiting.

Bill Hill didn't take his eyes from her. He heard Elwin say, ''Jesus Christ,'' reverently, like a prayer. Neither of them moved.

''I can see,'' Virginia said. ''I can see both of you plain as day.''

2

Bill Hill had to ring the doorbell to get into the Sacred Heart Rehabilitation Center, then had to explain why he wanted to see Father Quinn—about his good friend Elwin Worrel who'd been here and was drinking again—then had to wait while they looked for Quinn.

It was not like a hospital. The four-story building on the ghetto edge of downtown Detroit had once been a branch of the YWCA for black women, before integration, and that's what he decided it looked like, a YWCA.

He watched a man in pajamas, with slicked-back, wet-looking hair and round shoulders, go up to the reception desk where a young guy in a T-shirt and a good-looking black girl were on duty. The man in pajamas, feeling his jaw with his fingers, asked for some after-shave lotion. The young guy handed him a bottle of Skin Bracer. The man stuck his chin out, rubbed the Skin Bracer over his face and neck, and walked away, leaving the bottle on the counter. The young guy screwed the cap back on and put the bottle away somewhere.

Bill Hill strolled over and leaned against the counter. He said to the good-looking black girl, "Is Juvenal around?"

She said, "Juvenal?" a little surprised. The young guy in the T-shirt said, "I don't think he's here." He turned

11

to look at a schedule of names and dates tacked to the wall above the switchboard. "No, Juvie's off today."

Bill Hill said, "What's his last name again? I forgot it."

The good-looking black girl was quite thin and appealing in a sleeveless knit top, her little breasts pointing out. She said, "I don't know he has a last name."

"Are you in the program?" the young guy asked.

"You mean in AA?" Bill Hill said. "No, but this very close friend I mentioned is. Elwin Worrel? I met Juvenal over at Elwin's." Bill Hill waited.

It gave him a funny feeling. The two behind the counter seemed relaxed and friendly, not the least bit guarded; but to them he was an outsider. To be "in" here you had to be an alcoholic. The young guy said he could have a seat in there if he wanted and pointed to an empty reception room off the lobby where there was a piano, a fireplace, and hotel-lobby furniture that must've been sitting there thirty or forty years.

Bill Hill moved to the front windows of the reception room and looked out at the brewery that was across the Chrysler Freeway but seemed as near as next door. Above the red-brick complex was a giant sign that lit up red at night and said *Stroh's Beer* for all the alcoholics to see. It could make them thirsty, he bet. Or it could remind them of gutters and weeds and cold, vacant buildings. Bill Hill was wearing a yellow outfit today. Yellow-and-white-striped sport shirt, cream-yellow slacks, white belt, and white loafers. It was hot in here with no air conditioning. A dim, depressing place.

There he was, all yellow. And the priest appeared in a green-and-white warmup suit and sneakers. A couple of rays of sunshine in the musty old room, greeting each other by name, Bill Hill warming up, glancing at the windows and asking if that big Stroh's Beer sign was a temptation or a warning to the patients here. He meant to keep it light and chatty for a few minutes.

"The residents," Father Vaughan Quinn said, "they can look at the sign and think whatever they want, as long as they know they have three choices. Die, end up in a mental hospital, or quit drinking. It's their decision."

That wasn't keeping it light. Bill Hill said, "I'm afraid the only thing Elwin's trying to decide is which he likes better, Early Times or Jim Beam."

Another bad sign: the priest pushed up his sleeve to glance at his watch. He said, "Elwin's trouble, he knows he's an alcoholic, but he hasn't hit bottom hard enough to feel it."

That was a good lead. "Well, he's sure hitting other people fairly hard and doing a job on his house," Bill Hill said. He had a feeling he wasn't going to be asked to sit down, so he sank into a chair next to the big empty sofa, saying, "You know Virginia, Father?"

It was a mistake. The priest remained standing in his green-and-white outfit, gazing down at him now, a priest who played hockey and might've been a street fighter at one time. He could be a mean bugger, Bill Hill decided. A hip priest, graying hair over his ears, and with the look of a guy who could tell when you were bullshitting him, used to drunks lying to him, making excuses.

The priest said, "Sure, Virginia's been here."

There was a scar, forty-two stitches in his chin, from a blind-side meeting with a hockey puck, playing with the Flying Fathers. Bill Hill remembered that from the time he saw Father Quinn on a TV talk show.

"I understand she used to play the organ at your church," Quinn said.

See? The man knew things. Bill Hill smiled, shaking his head. "That was years ago."

"You're an ordained minister, aren't you?"

"I sell recreational vehicles, motor homes," Bill Hill

said. "No, but I used to have a church—Uni-Faith. Actually it was an outdoor setup . . . amphitheater could seat fifteen hundred, we had a chapel, a gift shop kinda like Stuckey's . . . but what drew the crowds, we had the world's tallest illuminated cross of Jesus, a hundred and seventeen feet high with 'Jesus Saves' at the top in blue neon you could see at night all the way from Interstate 75."

"Around here?" Quinn asked, interested.

"No, outside of Dalton, Georgia. I moved the whole show up here and went bankrupt. But that's another story."

"Fascinating," the priest said.

"Virginia was our organist—yeah, you knew that." Bill Hill paused. "You must also know she recovered her sight."

"I understand you were there when it happened," Quinn said.

"And a fella from the Center here by the name of Juvenal," Bill Hill said. "Virginia thinks he performed a miracle on her."

Quinn didn't seem startled or even change his expression. He said, "That's interesting, but what's a miracle? Some pretty amazing things happen around here all the time."

"I don't know," Bill Hill said, "it could've been a jolt to her head. Unless you think this fella did it laying on hands."

"Is that what he did?" Quinn asked.

"Well, I'm using that as a figure of speech. We had a young prayer healer at Uni-Faith, Reverend Bobby Forshay, used to lay on hands, so to speak. He wasn't too good at it. But something touched Virginia Worrel. Her face was clean before it happened; I saw it. Then when I looked at her after there was blood on it—around her eyes, on her forehead. You hear about that part, the blood?"

"Maybe it was from her nose. She touched her face and spread it around." Quinn pushed back the elastic cuff of his warmup jacket to glance at his watch.

"She wasn't bleeding from her nose. Virginia says she didn't have any cuts at all, not even in her scalp."

"How about a hemorrhage behind the eyes somewhere—I don't know, we're out of my area," the priest said. "You wanted to talk to me about Elwin, is that right?"

"Well, he's part of it," Bill Hill said. "This Juvenal's the other part. I wondered if you discussed it with him, about Virginia?"

"Listen, we're gonna have to make it another time," the priest said, starting to turn away. "We've got a volleyball game scheduled and I'm late as it is."

"Maybe I could talk to Juvenal—"

"Sure, any time."

"You can understand, Father. A woman, a good friend of mine, was blind fifteen years and now she can see. Juvenal was there a few minutes—I saw him sit down on the couch with her—then he was gone. How come? Did he witness her sight restored and it scared him or what?"

"You'll have to ask him that." The priest was moving off. "He'll be glad to talk to you."

"They said he's not here today." Bill Hill was pulling himself out of the chair now.

"Come back any time." Quinn paused in the doorway. "And, hey, if you've got any clothes you don't need, bring 'em along. You look like a pretty snappy dresser."

Shit, Bill Hill said, standing alone in that dim reception room. A pretty snappy dresser.

He came back to the Center the next day with two doubleknit leisure suits and a pile of sport shirts, some

hardly ever worn. He buzzed and they let him in, glad to
see him again. They were sorry though, Father Quinn was
in Toronto and Juvie was up in detox with a new arrival.
Bill Hill waited more than an hour. When the switchboard checked detox, Juvie was gone and no one seemed
to know where.

On the third visit Father Quinn was back from Toronto,
but was out for the day, not expected to return until late.
Juvie was around somewhere, they'd try to locate him.
But somehow never did.

The place wasn't that big. Four floors including a gym
and a swimming pool.

The day of Bill Hill's fourth visit Father Quinn was
getting ready for a board of directors meeting. Juvie was
out on a call; it would be hard to say when he'd be back.

Bill Hill said to the good-looking black girl, "You
know what it's like, the feeling people are avoiding you?"

"Tell me about it," the black girl said.

"I don't know what it is," Bill Hill said, "everybody
here's so nice and cooperative. But I don't seem to be
getting anywhere." He leaned against the counter, tired.

"Some days are like that," the black girl said. "I know
you been coming here—I'd like to give you Juvie's phone
number but, you understand, anonymity is part of the
deal, why it's called Alcoholics Anonymous?"

"You know him very well?"

"I'm not gonna tell you anything," the black girl said,
"so don't ask."

But why not? Waiting around, Bill Hill would begin to
lose interest and then something like this—why all the
mystery?—would perk him up. Why was Juvenal hiding
from him?

He said, "Let me ask you a straight question, okay?
How does a person get in this place? I mean an
alcoholic."

"Put your name in, get on the waiting list."

"The waiting list—what if you're in bad shape?"

"They're all in bad shape," the black girl said. "But we're full up, hundred and thirty-seven as of today."

"How about, do you take women?"

"Yeah, there some women. Some young girls even."

"Is that right? How long's the wait?"

"About three or four weeks. Unless somebody comes and they're desperate, I mean *really* in bad shape," the black girl said. "We don't turn people away, anything like that."

"I hope not," Bill Hill said.

Was he learning anything? Maybe. He was tired of waiting around. What he felt like right now was a drink.

He stopped off at the Athens Bar in Greektown and called Lynn Faulkner. The phone rang seven times. When she answered, Bill Hill said, "You know something, this is the first time I haven't had to talk to that recording. You know what it's like talking to somebody that isn't there?"

"Say it," Lynn Faulkner said, "I'm in the tub. I wasn't even gonna answer."

"You got a phone in there with you?"

"Listen, you want to call me back? I'm afraid I'm gonna get electrocuted."

"Get dressed and I'll take you out to dinner."

"Can't do it. I just got finished with Artie and a bunch of shitheads from L.A. and I'm not putting shoes on for anybody."

"Well, you're gonna have a couple, aren't you? Help you relax?"

"How come those guys in the business, no matter where they're from they all sound like they're from New York?"

"What guys?"

"You can bring some Asti Spumante if you want," Lynn said. "Cold, okay?"

"Now you're talking," Bill Hill said. "I got something interesting to tell you about. In fact, listen, it could even change your life."

Bill Hill thought he was kidding.

3

Lynn Marie Faulkner left Uni-Faith in 1968, a few months before Bill Hill moved the 117-foot cross of Jesus from Dalton, Georgia, to Flat Rock, Michigan. Lynn didn't think too much of living up north. Burrr, she said, too cold for a Miami girl. Lynn had a lot of cute ways about her then.

The reason she left Uni-Faith though, age nineteen and at the peak of her baton-twirling career, was to marry Doug "Whiz" Whaley, veteran saddle bronc rider with the Longhorn World Championship Rodeo. It was funny that when she finally divorced Doug last year—1976 being a year she would always remember—the rodeo was in Michigan, performing at the Pontiac Silverdome.

Doug Whaley, one-time saddle bronc rider turned calf roper, should have known the day would come. All he said, stepping into the Li'l Hobo travel trailer 2:30 in the afternoon and seeing no dishes and bread on the table, was, "Where's my dinner? You know I'm competing tonight."

He should have looked at his little girl first and tried softer words to get his chuck on the table. Instead, he walked into it dumb arrogant, head fuzzed with booze, and his peevish tone set off the charge.

19

Lynn said, "That's all, buddy. You get the trailer and I take the car. That's the division of property, and if you don't like it come by Oakland County Circuit Court for the hearing. You can listen while I tell the judge what a first-prize asshole you've been eight out of the past eight and a half years.

Lynn already had a lawyer and the prospect of a job in the music business; so she decided to stay around and get a no-fault Michigan divorce. Once she'd made up her mind, there was no reason to change it or feel guilty. The situation was clear-cut.

Doug drank and he fooled around, not saving a whole lot for Lynn. He sat a horse and could look at a young girl and make her shiver. But behind that rawhide hell-rider image was usually a half-drunk, stove-up Absorbine Junior freak. Whiz the fiz in the sack, all talk and no action. Doug could take his limp pecker and his Li'l Hobo trailer and see if he could connect them up somewhere else; Lynn was through.

A lot of little things broke down their so-so marriage, nearly all under the heading of Doug's immaturity. While Doug was looking at himself in back-bar mirrors, Lynn was growing up. She read all the time: back issues of *National Geographic*, popular novels, *Ms, Viva, WWD, Rolling Stone*, books on self-improvement—how to free yourself of guilt, fear, resentments and find the real *you*—and, by some lucky turn, *The Portable Dorothy Parker*, the pages becoming limp and dog-eared as she learned, with relief, it was all right to laugh at most serious things. She found out she was a pretty bright girl besides having a nice nose and a perky little behind, way smarter than Doug and too alive and eager to be his Dale Evans. Lynn had to get out while she still had a future.

A PR man at the Pontiac Silverdome, a really nice guy, got her a job in the advertising department of *Creem*, "America's Only Rock 'n' Roll Magazine," located above some storefronts in Birmingham—a swanky little Detroit suburb—and not like any business offices she had ever seen or heard of, with people walking around barefoot in cutoffs and tank tops. It was fun being in the world of commerce and rock and roll. Lynn sold KMA Records on a third-cover, four-color, twelve-insertions deal, and KMA hired her away from *Creem* as their Detroit-office publicist and record plugger at seventeen five a year plus a car and expenses. She called up her old buddy and former boss, Bill Hill, told him about it, and said, "Hey, not bad for a little Uni-Faith baton twirler who didn't know her ass from a hymnbook. Neat, huh?" Bill Hill said, "Not bad at all, honey. It's nearly as much as I make and I'm old enough to be your uncle."

That was nine months ago, when Lynn Whaley first got the job with KMA Records out of L.A. and was using her maiden name again, Lynn Faulkner, without the Marie.

Seventeen five plus a car and expenses, it sounded great. Except there was no KMA Detroit office. She'd have to work out of her own place, with an answering service or message recorder.

Well, that was all right. Maybe even better. She got an apartment in Somerset—a suburban complex with swimming pools, tennis courts, and a golf course, supposedly full of swinging singles—two bedrooms and a balcony overlooking the ninth fairway for three ninety a month, half of which she could write off as a business expense.

The car was a dull green Chevy Nova they must have bought second-hand from the post office. Lynn had to buy an AM-FM radio out of her twenty-cents-a-mile allowance.

Lynn said to Artie Rapp, the KMA publicity director in from L.A., "I'm supposed to take DJs out in that turd?"

Artie Rapp said, "Take them where? To your place? They have cars. All you got to do is see that KMA releases are played on the air. Check Peaches, Harmony House, Korvettes, see that KMA releases get good display and're selling. Meet the different KMA artists when they come to the Motor City, get them interviewed and fixed up and all, and do a little advance work on concerts and special promotions. What do you need for that, a Rolls Silver Cloud?"

"What do you mean 'fixed up and all'?"

"Sources. A band comes to town, say the Night-stalkers," Artie Rapp said, "they got their roadies, their groupies, all that. But say they want some good Colom-bian. That's all I'm talking about. Or they need some equipment or where's the best ribs in town—shit like that, nothing big. A group's in town you spend a little extra time with them. Otherwise you're what, twenty-seven hundred miles from the home office working out of your own pad with a generous expense account. You know how many people in the business would trade places with you?"

"How many?" Lynn said.

"I'll tell you what. There any good places to eat in this town I'll treat you to a nice dinner," Artie Rapp said, with his feet on Lynn's glass coffee table. "But since we're here—huh?—and we're gonna be working together . . ."

Lynn could handle Artie and she got along fine with people in the business, the station music directors and DJs, because she came on straight and didn't waste time giving them a lot of shuck and jive to get a KMA release on their play lists. If she really liked the record she might hustle it with a little extra effort, but without ever getting hyper about it. Any payola arrangements, if they were made, were left to Artie. Lynn kept her nose clean, offered no inducements, and was not sleeping with any of

the local DJs. At twenty-nine going on thirty she was
older than most of the rock and roll DJs in town, but
didn't seem to turn any of them off, not even in this
youth-oriented business. Lynn had a neat nose, bedroom
eyes, and a slim little figure.

She wore her blond hair layered back and feathered
fairly short, pasted on twenty-dollar eyelashes, rubbed in
a cheek gloss for that natural look, and painted her nails
light brown. Artie told her she had a killer body, wishing
he could see it in person beneath the hip-huggers and
India cotton shirt. He'd demonstrate that she was just the
right size. See, at five eight he was the average height of
the American fighting man in World War II and his
mouth, look, was just even with Lynn's nose when she
had her clogs on. Artie maneuvered for nine months and
never made it.

DJs who wanted to get it on with Lynn would give her
a sleepy look in a hang-out bar and say, "You want to
get it on?"

Lynn might say, "I better tell you, I'm a very religious
person basically and when I do it I have to be in love or
it just doesn't work. I guess it's the way I was brought
up."

If the DJ pressed and said, "So let's fall in love,"
Lynn would say, "You know where it is? It's in the
grooves. That's the bottom line. If my record's any good
you'll play it and it'll sell and my balling you won't make
the least bit of difference, will it?"

The guys in the business found out the platter-chatter
hip approach wasn't going to make it with Lynn. She was
a very laid-back young lady, not some trendy little chick
who was easily impressed. Though she did have her weak
moments.

Lynn had an affair with a TV news man until his
hairdo, which was like a brownish-gray helmet, finally
unnerved her. They would smoke grass and thrash around

in bed half the afternoon and the guy would come out of it with every hair still glued in place for his six o'clock newscast. Lynn felt either she couldn't bring out the real person beneath the hard charm or there was none there to begin with.

She had an affair with a married station manager who was real. He'd stop by her apartment Monday and Thursday evenings and tell her about the crises at work and his tragic situation at home, married to an alcoholic. Lynn thought she liked him pretty much; but after a few weeks of listening to his troubles as he got half smashed and then going through a speedy routine in bed, she decided that *real* didn't necessarily mean interesting. What the guy needed was a mother or a psychiatrist.

Was she happy as a record promoter?

Well, she had this suburban apartment and a telephone extension cord that reached from the second-bedroom office all the way out to the balcony overlooking the golf course. She had a lot of crushed velvet and chrome and a six-by-six-foot blowup of Waylon Jennings's outlaw face over the couch (he wasn't even a KMA artist, he was RCA). And Artie had raised her after six months to twenty grand a year.

She did wish she represented more black funk—and maybe a little country on the R and B side, not the heartache country or the green-hills-down-home country—instead of all the punk rock KMA was putting out.

She wished she didn't have to smile so much. Being nice in business when you didn't feel like it made your face ache, not to mention being a terrible pain in the ass.

And she could easily pass on all the waiting around when KMA artists came in to do concerts.

First, they very seldom arrived when they were supposed to—especially the rockers, who had absolutely no sense of time—and she'd spend hours at Detroit Metro waiting for flights.

Then more waiting in motel suites, lobbies, waiting backstage in a squeeze of groupies and roadies, tripping over power cables, being ignored by the managers and reps, waiting for a door to open and stoned musicians to come out—

Yes, but how many ex-baton twirlers with only high school, two seasons with a religious revival show, and a nine-year hitch in a rodeo trailer made twenty grand a year and expenses?

Maybe not any. But maybe because that's the way ex-baton twirlers were. They couldn't stand waiting around for something to happen.

4

"Everybody's so serious and uptight," Lynn said, "like somebody in the next room's dying or having a baby and, Christ, all they're doing is representing a rock and roll band. I kept thinking, what am I doing here?"

"Making money," Bill Hill said. He stood by the sliding screen door to the balcony, looking out at the ninth fairway, empty, everybody probably in having their supper. "You know what my view is? The parking area out back of the building. How much you pay, about four hundred?"

"Three ninety." Lynn, on the couch, had her telephone on the glass coffee table next to the $4.99 bottle of Asti Spumante Bill Hill had brought. Lynn liked the $7.99 one better, but would probably be going back to Gallo white before too long.

"See, I could *tell* myself I was where I wanted to be. I could, you know, rationalize. But my stomach kept giving me signals. What're you doing here? Get out. Leave."

"Your stomach," Bill Hill said.

"My gut reaction, with all the hotshots, the agents, the road managers—they walk in a place, they take over. *I'm* the one set up the hospitality suite. I got the Heinekens, the vodka and mix, scotch, a nice cheese tray—"

"Where was this?"

"The Sheraton out by Pontiac. If they're playing at Pine Knob usually we get them in the Sheraton, if the group isn't on the hotel's shit list."

"What one was this? The group."

"The Cobras. Bunch of little shitheads, I think they were invented."

"I don't believe I ever heard of them," Bill Hill said.

"You have to be just into puberty," Lynn said. "They wear, you'd love them, they wear skintight sort of snake-skin jumpsuits open in front practically down to their pubic hair to show their white skinny bodies, I mean *white*, and platform shoes. Two brothers, Toby and Abbot, and four other creepy guys I think they got from an institution."

"Jesus," Bill Hill said.

"They're bad enough, but wait." Lynn took time to sip Spumante, light a cigarette, and ease back into the cran-berry crushed velvet couch. "Artie's there, but I'm the one that arranged everything. I've got a few people I know from record stores. I've got the press—I think some kids from a school paper, but who knows. Several disc jockeys, not big names, but good guys. And my prize, I've got Ken Calvert, the ABX music director, I had to *beg* to come. 'Please, Kenny, tape an interview and make me look good in front of all the L.A. shitheads.' The first time I've ever begged anybody in my life. Kenny says—he can't *stand* the Cobras, he throws up you even mention their name—but he says okay, he'll do it as a favor."

"Jesus," Bill Hill said.

"Ken's there, a couple of DJs, the retail people, the press, all the reps and roadies standing around drinking, eating the cheese—and the band, the fucking Cobras, won't come out of their room, this suite adjoining the hospitality suite. Toby, or it was Abbott, I don't know, comes out *once* in his bikini Jockeys scratching his balls, picks up about half the cheese on a fork and goes back in the room. I go over and knock on the door and this guy I've never seen before goes, honest to God, he goes, 'They got all the head they need, doll, come back later.' I go, 'Waita minute. Who're you? I didn't even *invite* you.' This guy's got the half-assed 'fro and the beads and all—you can't tell anybody apart. They all look like sword fighters. Their road manager goes, 'Oh, Lynn? This is Marty Hyphen'—or Hyman, something like that—'he's with William Morris.' Like hot shit, the guy's with William Morris. I tell them, 'Look, I've got all these people here. You see them? Those are all people who, believe it or not, came here to meet the Cobras. That's Ken Calvert from ABX; he's even gonna do an interview.' And the guy from William Morris goes, 'Fuck Ken Calvert, the guys don't want to talk to anybody.' Not their manager, their *agent*. The road manager, all he says is, 'Strokes and pokes, uh? It's the business.' The band, they're in there picking their toes and getting stoned, and you know why they won't talk to anybody? Because last night in Toledo their back-up band blew them off the stage.''

Bill Hill said, ''Really?'' He followed only part of what Lynn was saying, but he paid attention, seated comfortably now in crushed velvet and chrome with a vodka and bitter lemon, letting Lynn get it all out before he eased into the reason he was here.

''They're pissed and arrogant,'' Lynn was saying, ''because the band that opened the show played louder than they did. I said to the road manager, 'So cut the back-up band's power. I assumed you'd do that anyway.' See, the Cobras have to overpower, put the amps way up, since they have absolutely no talent at all. The William Morris guy goes, 'Don't worry about it. All you have to do, see about the grass and some candy.' What? I go, 'Candy?' He goes, 'Nose candy, dummy. They like to have a little gig after, you understand?' A little *gig*. 'Few grams of candy and some presentable-looking chickies, okay?' I can't believe it. Artie's nodding, 'Right, don't worry about it.' I go, 'Wait a minute. What about all these *people* here?' The

William Morris guy goes, 'Did I invite them? Check with us first, doll, before you make any plans.' The road manager, Artie, neither of them say a word. Grown men worried about these spoiled kids in the next room. I look at Artie. He goes, 'Well, they do have a sound check they got to make. Explain it to them, okay?' All these people waiting around, some of them hearing everything we're saying.''

"Terrible," Bill Hill said.

"They don't care. For some reason, in this business," Lynn said, "they all get egoed out. The band, especially punk rockers, the least thing happens they get little bugs up their ass and then they're pouty and arrogant. Either that or they're so wired you can't even communicate with them. I'm saying to myself all this time, what am I *doing* here?''

"I'd quit," Bill Hill said.

"I did."

"Come on." Bill Hill straightened, then relaxed, not wanting to look eager.

"Not in so many words. I said to the William Morris guy, 'You want some dope for a little *gig* after and presentable-looking chickies? You want interviews and appearances you can cancel and limos every place they go and somebody to talk to pissed-off hotel managers when they bust up the furniture and explain to people when the freaks aren't gonna show? Well, you handle it, asshole,' and I walked out. Artie followed me out to the car— 'Where you going? Come on, I need you. You can't leave now.' I go, 'Artie, you're all set. You got William Morris,' and drove away. If he fires me, I'll tell him I already quit. If he doesn't, I don't know, I'm gonna rest before I think about it.''

Bill Hill came over and poured Lynn more Spumante, waiting on the tired girl beneath the giant face of Waylon Jennings. She looked small, helpless. She had on cutoffs to show her slender legs and a blousy, scooped-neck T-shirt that said *Bob Marley and the Wailers* across the front.

He said, "Money isn't everything, is it? If your job irritates you."

"If you let it," Lynn said. "I read you don't have to worry or feel guilty or irritated if you don't want to."

"You can hide in the closet and not talk to anybody," Bill Hill said.

"No, it means some people aren't happy unless they're *un*happy. If you know that, it's like it isn't the job that irritates you, it's fighting the job. I mean I shouldn't blame the job. As that road manager says, strokes and pokes. If I can't cope then I should get out. Unless I like being unhappy and irritable."

"You know who's a happy girl?" Bill Hill said, going out to the kitchen with his empty glass. "Virginia Worrel."

"I know. She called me."

"She did?" Bill Hill stood at the see-through counter with the vodka in his hand, looking out at Lynn, tiny in that crushed velvet, no more than a bite for big Waylon behind her. "I didn't know you two were close."

"I think she called everybody she knows. Getting your sight restored, that's pretty heavy."

"She tell you about the guy, Juvenal?"

"When she wasn't asking me about makeup. She thinks I'm an expert. I told her all I use is a little gloss—"

"What'd she say about him?"

"—Show Stopper pink lipstick if I'm wearing light colors, I told her to try a little mascara. I remember Virginia had nice eyelashes. Then I tried to tell her how to apply it without mentioning, I don't know why, her eyes. Like if I said, 'Your eyes,' she'd be blind again. It was weird."

"What'd she say about Juvenal?"

"She said he was cute, very clean-cut looking. That'd be a switch, after all the freaks with the hair and the beads."

"You want to meet him?"

"I don't know. Why?"

"Virginia tell you she went to see him?"

"Yeah, they had coffee."

"I tried to see him four times," Bill Hill said. "But it was like they were keeping him hidden. Then right after I called you? I thought hell, I bet Virginia's seen him. So called her. Sure enough, she went to see him and they had quite a talk about one thing and another. But you know what's funny? See, Virginia believes he healed her—"

"Why not?" Lynn said. "That's more exciting than thinking it was your husband beating on you. That's one thing Doug never tried; he knew better."

"What I'm saying," Bill Hill said, still patient, "Virginia believes it, but this Juvenal never claimed he did or he didn't. She said he avoided it, but without being obvious. He was sort of funny and never got too serious."

Lynn was nodding. "She said he was cute and she said he made her feel good."

"She mentioned that. Made her feel good—"

"Like he was very warm and sensitive and cared about her," Lynn said, "how she was. Not from the words he used especially, I mean what he said, but it was the feeling she got. She felt like, alive."

"That's interesting, isn't it?" Bill Hill said. "She said she had the feeling he knew things about her she hadn't told him."

"She mentioned that," Lynn said.

"She tell you he spent some time in a monastery?"

"I don't think so."

"He was a Franciscan monk for about ten years. She tell you he was a missionary down on the Amazon River in Brazil?"

"Never mentioned it."

"Came back after about four years," Bill Hill said,

"spent some time in a seminary here and then quit the order."

"He did?"

"Quits the Franciscans and goes to work at an alcohol rehabilitation center. He wasn't a priest, he was a brother, so I guess it was easier for him to quit. But if he's into this brotherhood work, being a missionary and all, why would he quit the order?"

"I don't know," Lynn said. "Maybe something about it irritated him, you know? Maybe they were real strict and didn't let him do what he liked doing. Say, he wanted to work in the hospital and they put him in an office or something. Like Audrey Hepburn in *The Nun's Story* finally got pissed off at the mother superior or somebody and left."

"I was thinking along those lines," Bill Hill said. "Like what if down in Brazil he was healing people and they didn't want him to, so they sent him home."

"Why wouldn't they want him to?"

"If the head Franciscan was jealous of him, or they thought it would cause too much of a commotion. People coming from all over to get cured, it could interfere with the work they're doing converting natives. Pretty soon they're setting up stands to sell Juvie religious items—"

Lynn started to grin.

"What's the matter?" Bill Hill said.

"Now we're getting to it, aren't we?"

"I'm saying they could've been afraid of commercializing religion or a cult developing, the ignorant natives holding him up as a saint, even worshipping him. You see what I mean?"

"I ought to. I worked for you long enough."

"I'm talking about something different."

"I know," Lynn said, "you're talking about the real thing, not Reverend Bobby Forshay down out of the piny woods. God, Bobby used to make me nervous. He was always trying to get me in his motel room or off someplace. He was spooky, you know it?"

"You asked me— All right," Bill Hill said, "maybe just maybe, this Juvenal is the real article. What would you think of that?"

"I don't know," Lynn said. "What if he is?"

"Do you believe he can actually heal people?"

"I guess. I don't know, funny things happen I don't understand. I believe, I don't know how, but I believe even Bobby Forshay actually healed a few people, once he got it in his head he could do it."

There, that's what he wanted to hear. Bill Hill sat back on the couch nodding thoughtfully, not so much agreeing with what Lynn said, but happy to see she still believed in basic stuff, even after spending nearly a year in the world of rock and roll. She was still little Lynn Marie Faulkner beneath the Bob Marley T-shirt and the jive talk, your basic Florida Orange Bowl pageant girl and one-time Fundamentalist.

He said, "You believe in miracles?"

She said, "Sure. I think they're a good idea."

"How'd you like to get to know this Juvenal?"

"For what reason?"

"See if he's real."

"And if he is?" Lynn paused. "He was in the religious life once and he quit."

"Don't get ahead of me," Bill Hill said. "Right now I'm just curious. Aren't you?"

"You want to get out of the r.v. business, wasting your talent selling motor homes."

"Are you curious or not?"

"Maybe a little. I haven't met him yet."

He liked that word *yet*. Bill Hill said, "You understand why I can't do a study on him. The priest there at the Center knows all about Uni-Faith from Virginia, so he's suspicious, without coming right out and saying it. You got the anonymous part of AA to contend with; so nobody there'll give you even his last name. They're cheerful, very friendly, and they *sound* like they're trying to help you. But you get the feeling you're not gonna learn a thing unless you're in the club."

"What club?" Lynn said.

"AA."

She didn't see it yet and he wasn't going to rush her.

"I was thinking, how'd you like to join for a few days?"

Lynn said, "You know what I drink? Maybe two of these a week," nudging the Spumante bottle with her toe.

Bill Hill had his answer ready. "Yeah, but you got to watch Doug Whaley get smashed for ten years almost. How was he in the morning, pretty bad?"

"He was a mess. Carried on like he was gonna die till he had that first one."

"You could fake it, couldn't you? Act hung over, shake a little bit?"

"I'd never be able to throw up as well as Doug could."

"I was thinking," Bill Hill said, "you might even pretend to have some kind of ailment you tell this Juvenal about. See what he does."

He took his time, letting Lynn fool with the idea. It was still early, still quite light outside at twenty to eight, a restful time of the day.

"I don't know," Lynn said, "it seems like it'd be a waste of time. I find out he's a faith healer, so what? You're not in the business anymore."

"Does he have the power?" Bill Hill said. "If he does, why's he hiding, keeping it a secret? That's what intrigues me about it. Like Virginia says, there's something there you *feel* when you're with him, and I want to know what it is."

Lynn was thoughtful, off somewhere. "Pretend I have some kind of ailment? Like what?"

"Well, if you're an alcoholic it could be gastritis, I

suppose ulcers, a bad liver. Didn't Bobby Forshay cure you one time?"

"That was sugar diabetes. But I couldn't pull something like that, I mean that they could check on and see I don't have."

"We'll think of something." Bill Hill wasn't worried about a detail. He had thought it was going to take more persuading and convincing, but he was almost home.

"It might be kinda fun," Lynn said. "Different anyway, huh?"

"Say, intellectually interesting," Bill Hill said, "even if it doesn't make us a dime."

She was silent again.

"What's the place like, a rest home?"

"You could say that."

"How would I get in, just tell them I'm an alcoholic?"

"It takes a little more than that. Usually there's a wait—"

"How long?"

"—unless the person that comes is in really bad shape." Bill Hill smiled at Lynn. "Have another drink, honey. Finish the bottle and we'll get you another. Though I think it'd be quicker if you switched to vodka, and you won't be so thirsty in the morning."

"You mean tonight?" Lynn was pushing herself up out of the crushed velvet. "You want me to go in there smashed?"

"They won't think anything of it," Bill Hill said.

5

August Murray said later that outside of himself and of course the twenty from the Gray Army of the Holy Ghost, practically everybody in the courtroom was black. He said, "You want to see a profile of Detroit, go down to Recorder's Court in the Frank Murphy Hall of *in*-Justice."

The court clerk, sitting at a counter in front of the judge's bench, was black. A police sergeant, the bailiff, next to the clerk, was black. There were black probation people and skinny black policewomen with shoulderbags, three black defense lawyers, a young white-girl defense lawyer trying to prove something, another blond girl recording the cases, and a two-hour line—while August Murray waited his turn—of black prostitutes, black shoplifters, black guys who beat up their common-law wives, black people charged with larceny under a hundred dollars, assault and battery, indecent exposure—maybe there were a few white people. Judge Kinsella was swarthy turning gray, supposedly white. The assistant prosecutor under all the hair looked like some kind of hybrid. Black voices—a girl saying, "I'm already doing sixteen to two out to the House." Sullen or half asleep, very few of the voices addressed the court as "Your Honor" or had much to offer in their defense. The voices made sounds. August Murray—waiting through all that, until the court clerk called file number 7753047 and his name—would have a few things to say.

He stood at the microphone facing the clerk's counter and the judge's bench and waited another five minutes, at least, staring at the judge, trying to get his eye. The judge was talking to a black policewoman, signing a paper, having her swear to something with her hand raised. A black lawyer was leaning on the counter talking to the clerk now. The police sergeant next to the clerk said, "You people back there, take a seat."

Murray wanted to look around, but kept staring at the judge, waiting for the judge to look up and notice all the young white men in the courtroom, twenty of them among the black relatives of the defendants, all wearing light gray armbands and six of them carrying cardboard signs, turned in, they would hold up at the right time. August Murray wore a long-sleeved brown sport shirt, a white T-shirt showing beneath the open collar. He carried a silver pen and pencil set and two Magic Markers, a red one and a blue one, clipped to his shirt pocket. Around his left bicep was the armband of the Gray Army of the Holy Ghost, a soaring white dove appliquéd on a field of light gray felt. He kept waiting for the judge to notice his armband and become aware of all the other armbands in the courtroom.

But when the judge did look up he didn't seem to notice.

August Murray stood at parade rest, his brown crepe-soled shoes exactly eighteen inches apart, right hand holding his left wrist behind his back. He would maintain this stance throughout the proceeding.

The court clerk said, "Mr. Murray, you're charged with assault and battery—" He looked down at the counter again and said something to the police sergeant next to him. Their heads remained together looking down

at the file, the clerk turning a page and turning it back
again.

August Murray, staring at the clerk now, was sure they
were doing it on purpose. He said to the clerk in his
mind, Look at me. *Look* at me.

Dark hair in place, combed straight back; no sideburns
or excess hair on his face. Clean. Serious. Not about to
take any second-class treatment or be shuffled, pushed
aside. The clerk would know immediately when he looked
at him—

"Albert—Father Albert Navaroli," the clerk said. "Is
Father Navaroli in the courtroom?"

He was here. Murray had seen the little guinea priest
in the hall. The hippie guinea priest and another priest.

The police sergeant held up his hand. "Come up here
please, Father."

Please, Father— The cop had said to Murray, "Stand
right there." Judged before a word was said, who was
right and who was wrong. Nothing had changed at the
Hall of in-Justice.

The clerk said to Murray, "Are you represented by
counsel?"

Murray said, "I represent myself."

Then a conference between the clerk and the judge
before the clerk sat down again and the young assistant
prosecutor with his hair touching his suit coat said to the
hippie, curly-haired street priest, "Father Navaroli, would
you tell us what happened, please?"

Murray glanced at the priest then. He was shorter than
August Murray's five seven and a half, even with all his
curly hair. The priest was wearing a black suit with a
Roman collar. At his mass the priest had worn vestments
that looked like they'd been made for some kind of an
Indian ceremony, with fringe and a beaded stole.

The priest said, "Well, it was during the ten o'clock

mass, right after the offertory. We were singing the Sanctus—''

"The *what?*'' August Murray said. "You were singing Holy, Holy, Holy.''

"Mr. Murray—'' the assistant prosecutor began.

"I'm asking him a question as the right of counsel,'' Murray said.

The judge spoke for the first time, calmly. He said, "If you're representing yourself you can cross-examine. But when your turn comes.''

A quiet putdown. Murray stared at the judge and watched him look away.

There were other interruptions. People coming up and whispering to the clerk, to the judge, the judge talking to someone and not paying any attention as the priest continued.

"This man, Mr. Murray,'' the priest said, "came in with several others and began distributing pamphlets right up the main aisle when I saw them, disturbing the people hearing mass—''

"*Mass?*'' August Murray said. "That was a mass?''

"Mr. Murray,'' the assistant prosecutor said, "you've already been told—''

"It didn't look like a mass to me,'' Murray said, staring at the judge. "Guitars, tamborines. I thought maybe it was a square dance.'' He smiled a little now, testing the judge. "You know what I mean, Your Honor? Some kind of a new-wave Vatican II hoedown.''

The judge didn't smile or respond and the prosecutor, as though in pain, shook his head and told Murray to be quiet during Father Navaroli's testimony. Not *please* be quiet. Murray kept his hands behind his back, not moving, knowing his people in the audience, scattered through the semicircle of benches, were there waiting.

The curly-haired priest said he addressed Mr. Murray and his group from the altar, asking them to kindly take a pew or else leave the church, as they had not been authorized to distribute literature. Murray approached him, the priest said, and began yelling, using abusive language.

"What exactly did he say?" the prosecutor said.

The clerk looked at the wall clock above the door and then at his watch. The judge seemed deep in thought.

"Did he place his hands on you?" the prosecutor added.

The priest cleared his throat. "He said, Mr. Murray said, 'This is not the holy sacrifice of the mass. This is a clown show, a mockery, and a sacrilege.' Then he pushed his pamphlets at me, trying to get me to take them. The pamphlets fell—"

"He knocked them out of my hands," Murray said.

"He grabbed my stole and tried to pull it off," the priest said. "I caught the end of the stole and pulled, like a tug-a-war, and that's when he pushed me with both hands, hard, knocking me down."

"He tripped on his microphone cord," Murray said.

The judge was looking at him now, finally, about to get into it. He said, "One more interruption, Mr. Murray, and I'm holding you in contempt of court—"

"Sir?"

"You're trying for one hundred dollars or ten days in the Wayne County Jail." The judge seemed to pause, finally noticing Murray's armband.

Murray grinned, giving the judge a sheepish, little-kid look. "You mean just for saying, 'Sir,' Your Honor?"

"If you interrupt testimony again." Now the judge was studying the file in front of him. He looked up, saying, "Have you been in trouble before this?"

Murray shook his head. "No, Your Honor."

The assistant prosecutor said, "He's got two priors. Assault and disorderly conduct."

The judge was looking at Murray, waiting.

Murray said, "You asked if I'd been in trouble,"

trying the little-kid grin again. "I didn't consider those charges much trouble, Your Honor. I was put on probation."

"For the assault," the clerk said. "He violated his probation with the disorderly and was fined two hundred dollars, November 1976."

"You don't consider that being in trouble?" the judge asked.

"Your Honor," Murray said, "are you asking me to testify against myself?"

The clerk saw it coming. He looked at the clock again and sat back in his chair, glancing at the police sergeant. The young assistant prosecutor made a little turn with his hands in his pockets, walked over to his table. Judge Kinsella seemed tired, though it was only 11:15 in the morning.

He said, "The court requests you answer questions that are a matter of record."

"If it's in the records," Murray said, still calm though not grinning now, "why ask the question? Unless it's to trap me. You asked if I'd been in trouble before. I said no, I didn't consider it trouble. Did I answer your question or not?"

The clerk turned, half rising to have a conference with the judge. Murray didn't mind the wait now; he had them irked and edgy.

He said, "Your Honor?"

But the judge didn't look up.

"Your Honor?"

Now he did. "Wait till we're finished here."

"I just want to say I think it's open to question whether you're qualified, Your Honor, to sit in judgment on this particular hearing—"

The judge was staring now, yes, eyes fixed, brought to attention; the clerk turning back again as Murray delivered his statement in a dry, unhurried tone.

"—considering the fact you've been excommunicated from the Church, Your Honor, following your recent divorce and, if I'm not mistaken, remarriage? Since this is basically a religious question we're talking about here—"

The judge seemed to be getting hold of himself, formulating his words, or counting to ten. He said, then, "No, the question is whether or not you are in contempt of this court—"

"Your Honor, I feel the judgment of an excommunicated Catholic layman could be prejudicial in examining *my* right to defend *my* church and its sacred traditions from a carnival atmosphere that one *not* in the Church any longer might fail to recognize." Murray paused, giving the judge a chance to speak.

"I've been patient with you. I feel I've indicated sufficient warning—"

That was enough.

"Let me say, Your Honor," Murray began again, "I believe you should disqualify yourself on prejudicial grounds and appoint a judge not subjectively concerned."

"Mr. Murray"—the judge's tone was brittle, controlled with an effort—"this is a misdemeanor court hearing on a charge of assault and battery. You will not open your mouth again unless I give you permission. Is that clear?"

"I want the record to show, Your Honor, that you are now speaking in a subjective and emotional fit of anger—"

"You're in contempt!" The judge cut him off, straightening as if to rise out of his high-backed leather chair. "And will be remanded to the custody of the bailiff!"

"I want a jury trial," Murray said. "God help me, in another court. It's my right and you know it."

Now. Murray unlocked his hands, bringing them to his sides. He saw the judge's gaze rise suddenly and the police sergeant come to his feet, hand going to his holstered revolver.

''You gonna shoot them?'' Murray said.

The signs were up now, he knew, he could feel them before he glanced over his shoulder to see the words, red on white squares of cardboard, OUTRAGE . . . OUTRAGE . . . OUTRAGE . . . OUTRAGE . . . OUTRAGE . . . OUTRAGE, six of them held high, scattered through the courtroom, and the twenty members of the Gray Army of the Holy Ghost standing now, silently facing the court.

''Go ahead,'' Murray said to the police sergeant, ''shoot them.''

6

A little gray-haired woman in a sleeveless yellow blouse brought Lynn a breakfast tray at 7:30. She said, "How you doing? I'm Edith, I'm your Big Sister."

Lynn could smell oatmeal. She said, "Where am I?"

"You're in detox. Don't you remember coming here?"

"I mean where *am* I?"

Lynn was still wearing her scooped-neck Bob Marley and the Wailers T-shirt and cutoffs. She sat up in the single bed, thinking of an orphanage, not a hospital. She had pictured white walls and hospital beds. The walls were pale green and needed paint. The two empty beds in the room, made up, were covered with faded summer spreads. Sunlight came in the window through a heavy-gauge wire screen. The place was old, an institution.

"Few days, once you get dried out, they'll move you up to four," the little gray-haired woman said. "I'll take you around, help you get some other things if you want. I don't see a suitcase anywhere—"

"I'm at Sacred Heart, huh?" Lynn said, practicing, trying to sound foggy and vague. Her head was fairly clear though it throbbed and she was nauseated. She could remember one hangover before this, years and years ago, and hadn't had anything to drink for weeks.

"There was a bar—I was sitting there talking to a friend about getting straightened out—"

She had not worn her eyelashes or skin gloss, but had rubbed on a dark red shade of lipstick Bill Hill said would make her look pale, left the apartment about 2:30 A.M. after two and a half bottles of Spumante—giggling, telling him she was going to walk in naked, liven the place up—and had been dropped off in front of the Center with Bill Hill's parting words, "Ring the bell then quick see if you can throw up a little."

"Your friend done you a favor," the little gray-haired woman said. "You don't look too bad except maybe your eyes."

The doctor asked how long she had been drinking. Lynn said, oh, about ten years. She said lately she'd been drinking about a gallon of wine a day and carried a pint of vodka in her purse just in case. The doctor didn't seem impressed.

The nurse, taking blood samples, asked if she'd been eating regularly. Lynn said, oh, you know, now and then. The nurse said well, she didn't look too bad, considering.

What was this, not too *bad?* Compared to the other women wandering around here, with their bruised white skin and circles and oily hair, she looked like a homecoming queen.

The nice woman counselor, sitting at her metal desk smoking cigarettes (everybody here, Lynn decided later, smoked two packs a day), asked if she remembered coming. Lynn said, vaguely.

"Have you experienced blackouts?"

"Some."

"For extended periods or just the night before?"

"I guess both."

"Do you think you're alcoholic?"

"I guess I must be, all I've been drinking."

The woman counselor said it wasn't the quantity that counted, it was the dependency. The first step was to realize she was powerless over alcohol, then learn to accept it, and finally substitute an entirely new attitude for the dependence.

"How?"

That would come. She'd see films on alcoholism, hear talks by recovering alcoholics working in the field and, once through orientation, take part in group sessions twice a day during the seventeen weeks of the program.

Seventeen *weeks?*

The woman counselor asked about her moods—any feelings of depression or anxiety?—to the point that Lynn was afraid the woman suspected something and was trying to trap her. When the phone rang and the woman counselor walked over to the window with the receiver, looking out as she spoke, her back to Lynn, Lynn looked at the steno pad on the desk and saw the notations, "Natural but somewhat evasive . . . Underlying feelings of guilt . . . Appearance not too bad."

When the counselor returned to her desk Lynn asked if she could use her phone after. The counselor explained that in order to concentrate on her immediate problem and not be concerned with anything else, Lynn would have no contacts outside the Center for the first five weeks.

"You mean I'm trapped here?"

"You can leave anytime you want," the counselor said, "but if you stay you have to play by the house rules."

"I thought the door was locked."

"To keep friends and relatives and all their good intentions, and all your old problems, out," the counselor said, "not to keep you in."

Lynn felt better, but tried not to show it.

She studied a crucifix on the wall: a pale plaster Jesus

on a varnished cross, the figure contorted, eyes raised in agony. Dramatic, but was it necessary? She liked plain crosses better, without the figure.

Lynn's gaze moved to a blown-up photograph of an empty room littered with old newspapers and junk, the hall or lobby of a condemned building where street bums would find shelter.

Lynn said, "Is that this place before it was fixed up?"

The man sitting next to her in the booth, stirring his coffee, said, "I don't know what it's supposed to be. Looks like some dump on Michigan Avenue."

Maybe the photograph hung on the wall as a reminder, or an option. Huddle in that filthy place sweating or shivering, or both; or relax here in the coffee shop of the Sacred Heart Center, second floor, across from the TV lounge. There were tables, booths along the windowed wall that looked down on the backyard and the volleyball court; soft-drink, cigarette, and candy vending machines and a pair of sixty-cup coffee urns with trays of cups, cream pitchers, and packets of sugar. The coffee was free, very strong, and all you wanted.

Lynn had eaten lunch, sat through an orientation session, watched a film called *Bourbon in Suburbia*, and had been in the coffee shop nearly an hour, wondering if she should ask about Juvenal, look for him, or wait until they happened to meet. It was kind of interesting watching people, sizing them up.

They used a lot of cream and sugar and ate candy, passing around a box of butter mints, and smoked cigarettes. Some of the men rolled their own and, at first, Lynn thought they were making joints, but it was Bugle pipe tobacco, a blue package they rolled up and shoved into their back pockets. People, the residents, sat around awhile and left and others came in—

Considerably more men than women, a few black people, which, for some reason, surprised Lynn. A good-looking black girl with a cute figure. Two tables of bridge. It was hot in the room, even with the windows open. Looking down at the yard she saw a younger group sitting in the sun, on a bench and the grass nearby, four boys with their shirts off—actually young men in their twenties—and a girl wearing cutoffs and a halter top.

The little gray-haired woman, Edith, sitting across from Lynn, said, "They got the problem, you know it? Oh, there's plenty of others, I don't mean you have to be a hippie or anything. But drugs *and* booze, that's the killer. You notice they don't give you any tranquilizers here unless you're climbing up the wall."

The man next to Lynn told them how many Valium he used to take a day; sometimes six, eight, plus a couple of fifths.

Lynn said she wondered if the Stroh's Beer sign across the freeway bothered anybody, tempted them.

The man sitting next to her said it didn't bother him none; beer always gave him a headache.

Edith would stop people and introduce them to Lynn, saying, almost proudly, "She only come in last night." As though look, she's better already. "I'm her Big Sister."

A skinny, hunch-shouldered man said he came in three days ago, fella told him he was his Big Brother and he hadn't seen the son of a bitch since. Edith was concerned and told him he should talk to a counselor. The skinny, hunch-shouldered man said he wanted to call Wayne County Social Service, but they wouldn't let him. He said how was he supposed to get his check if they didn't know where he was?

There were a number of those skinny, hillbilly-looking guys, recent skid-row graduates who still looked soiled and wore second-hand clothes that hung on them. What happened to guys' asses who drank too much? But there, playing bridge, was a man who had to be an executive of some kind, distinguished, even with his florid Irish face and little slit of a mouth. Now *there* was an alcoholic. But if that was the look, what about the black guy with the beard and the yellow tank top? Or the fat girl in the Big Mac bib overalls, awful hair, sitting with the blond lady in the designer blouse and white earrings? There was no obvious type, and yet all were aware of something Lynn would never understand. No matter how well she faked it she would still feel left out as they smiled and shook their heads and talked among themselves, passing time, hopefully saving their lives.

It was interesting. Then less interesting, thinking, What am I doing here? Quit fooling around and go look for the guy, Juvenal. Except she didn't want to appear to know anything about him. She didn't want to ask for him—

As it turned out, she didn't have to.

Lynn had a feeling—it was strange—the moment she saw him come in and begin talking to people, touching shoulders, moving from table to table on his way to the coffee urns, she knew it was Juvenal: not from Virginia's or Bill Hill's description, but as if she had known him from some time before, when they were little kids, and recognized him now, grown up but not changed that much.

He had a boyish look, light brown hair down on his forehead, slim body in a blue-and-red striped knit shirt and jeans. Very friendly, the outgoing type—and yet he seemed a little shy. Was that it? No, not shy. What it was, he seemed genuinely glad to see everybody but was quiet about it, natural. Maybe a little naive? No, it was more like he was unaware of himself. That would be a switch, Lynn thought, a guy who's the center of attention not trying to act cool or entertaining or anything. People were getting up and leaving, but stopping to say hello to him.

Edith, her Big Sister, said, "Oh, shit, I got to meet

with my group. I shouldn't say that, it's doing me a world
of good, but I get tired of thinking all the time, trying to
say how I feel.''

The man next to Lynn said, ''Quit your bitching,
you're sober, aren't you?'' He got up with his empty cup
and left.

Lynn was alone in the booth by the time Juvenal got
his cup of coffee, looked around the room, and came over
to her.

He said, ''Can I join you?''

''Sure.''

''You're Lynn, aren't you?''

''Yeah. How'd you know?''

He slid in across from her. ''I'm Juvenal—on the staff
here. You came in this morning early . . .'' He paused,
staring at her with a warm expression, nice brown eyes,
super eyelashes.

She wanted to ask him if they were real.

He said, ''You look great. You know it?''

It stopped her. ''Oh—do you think so?''

''How do you feel?''

''Not too bad. A little, you know, fuzzy.''

''Your eyes are clear.'' He smiled and there was the
innocent look. ''You have very pretty eyes.''

''Wow,'' Lynn said, ''all the compliments. I'm not
used to it.''

''You don't look like you've been drinking, I mean too
heavily.''

''I thought the amount isn't what you go by.''

''No, but after a while it shows.'' He smiled again.
''What're you doing here, hiding?''

''From what?''

''I don't know. That's why I'm asking.''

Lynn hesitated. ''I thought you were being funny.''

''No, I'm curious. What're you doing here?''

''Isn't this a place you dry out?''

"You're not an alcoholic," Juvenal said.

"That's funny, the doctor didn't question it, or the nurse, or my counselor."

"Come on, tell me."

Looking at his eyes, into his eyes, she felt strangely moved and wanted to say, I can see you in there, I know you.

What she said was, "You've got it turned around," not believing she was saying it, but knowing she had to be honest with him and not play games or try to put something over on him. "You're the one that's hiding. I came here to find you."

"Oh, no. Oh, Christ," Father Quinn said. They had seen him and there was nothing he could do but continue along the short hall to the lobby where the right-winger was waiting, the right-winger with a folded newspaper under his arm and a seedy old priest it looked as though the right-winger was delivering.

Father Quinn did not like August Murray. He considered him a pain in the ass and a humorless bore; Christ, anyone who could get excited about bringing Latin back to the Church. But August Murray—since the first time he had visited a few months ago—had been bringing bundles of used clothing, showing an interest in the Center, though he seemed to have little or no understanding of drunks. He was weird, but he was a do-gooder, so Father Quinn tolerated him, let him do some good.

August said, "Father, I want you to meet Father Nestor. He's a Franciscan. Or he was until recently."

An old man in an old black suit, a limp fringe of gray hair and practically no grip to his handshake. The priest said, "How do you do." The corners of his mouth looked sticky.

"Father Nestor's pastor out at Saint John Bosco in Almont. You know where Almont is, Father?"

Quinn said no, but he was happy to meet Father Nestor. It was a part of the work he had to put up with, being civil.

August said, "It's out toward Lapeer, northeast. Father Nestor—I've been telling him about the Center and he took up a special collection last Sunday at mass he wants to give you."

The old priest was holding a manila envelope with both hands.

Strange. Quinn said, "Well, we certainly appreciate it, Father." But it was strange, a contribution from a parish he'd never heard of.

"We collected eighty-two dollars," Father Nestor said.

And Quinn was thinking, That must be some parish. August Murray was saying, "I told Father you'd take a few minutes of your time to tell him about your work here. I'm gonna run upstairs and say hello to Juvie." He was already moving away.

"He might be out," Quinn said.

"No, I called. He knows I'm coming." Going toward the stairway now that rose next to the elevator.

"August"—trying to sound pleasant—"don't bother him if he's in detox, all right?"

"I know where he'll be," August Murray said. He went up the stairs, past an empty bird cage on the landing, and made the turn to the second floor.

"Let me ask you something first," Lynn said. "Did you ever live in Miami?"

"Uh-unh."

"Dalton, Georgia?"

"Nope."

"And you were never with the rodeo— I don't know

why, I have a feeling we used to know each other. I don't mean we met one time, I mean we *knew* each other.''

"You're a friend of Virginia's," Juvenal said. "Another friend of hers's been coming here."

"That's Bill Hill. Virginia and I both used to work for him."

"And he put you up to it," Juvenal said. "Why?"

"See if you're real."

"I'm real. I'm sitting here with you."

"You know what I mean."

"You want to know if I can actually heal people, perform miracles?"

"I don't have any reason to doubt it," Lynn said, "but it's a lot to believe, isn't it? See, the last miracle worker I knew was always trying to get me in his room."

Juvenal, grinning, seemed to appreciate that. Then, for a moment, looking past her, the smile left his face. It was gone and then back again, though not with the same warmth and intensity, and he raised his hand to wave someone over.

Lynn looked around, surprised to see the room nearly empty. A man with his hair combed straight back was coming toward the booth. He had a row of pencils or pens in his shirt pocket and was carrying a newspaper, taking it from under his arm.

Juvenal said, "August, this is Lynn. Have a cup with us."

"I don't drink coffee," August Murray said. He glanced at Lynn, nodding, and laid the newspaper open in front of Juvenal.

"Now what'd you do?" Juvenal said.

"Right there, with the picture."

"Doesn't look like you," Juvenal said.

"It was taken four years ago at Kennedy Square. We were counterdemonstrating against some hippie peace march."

Lynn moved over. Juvenal was studying the paper spread open on the table and August didn't seem to know where to sit. He slid in next to Lynn, but didn't look at her. He watched Juvenal reading the news story, Juvenal smiling a little. Lynn was thinking that August was about the squarest-looking guy she'd ever seen. She hoped he wasn't a good friend of Juvenal.

Lynn said, "How're you doing? August, is it?"

He said that's right, showing absolutely no interest. She could be sitting at another table.

Juvenal brought her in. He looked up and said, "August is head of a group called Outrage and they demonstrate a lot. This is about him getting arrested." He looked down at the paper again. "What was it, disturbing the peace?"

"Assault," August said.

"Yeah, I see it. You hit this . . . Father Navaroli?"

"I didn't hit him, I tried to hand him some pamphlets."

"And you told the judge he wasn't qualified?"

"He's a dumb guinea fallen-away, excommunicated Catholic. What does he know? It was like they were having a trial instead of a hearing. I said, 'Wait a minute. Nobody's bothered to ask me, but I want a *jury* trial.' You understand, when it's just a misdemeanor they don't like to take time, but I knew I could demand it and I did, a twelve-man jury trial."

Lynn looked from one to the other, from August, very serious, to Juvenal, amused.

Something didn't seem right. If Juvenal had been in a religious order, not a priest but close to it, why did he think this was funny? Look at it another way, if Juvenal thought it was funny, why didn't August?

Lynn said, "Outrage is the name of your group?"

"Organization uniting—" Juvenal began. "What is it, August?"

"Organization Unifying Traditional Rites As God Expects."

"They go around breaking up guitar masses," Juvenal said.

"That's quite an oversimplification." August seemed offended. "Our purpose, as you well know, is to restore traditional forms of worship."

"As God expects," Juvenal said.

"As handed down for two thousand years from Christ and the Apostles," August said.

Juvenal looked at Lynn. "Are you Catholic?"

"No, but I was married to sort of one," Lynn said. "Except he never went to church. I know what you're talking about, but I don't know much about it."

"August likes Latin," Juvenal said. "He doesn't like the mass in English. Or peace marches or Communists."

"I don't know any Communists," Lynn said, "but I met a guy from William Morris who's a fascist."

"They're different," Juvenal said. "I've met some fascists myself, in some pretty unexpected places."

"They're very serious," Lynn said. And made a face, hunching her shoulders, aware of August next to her.

Juvenal caught it, smiling, shaking his head. August didn't react, or wasn't listening. He said, "You say *I* don't like the mass in English. Listen, we have at least two hundred thousand followers in the United States we're sure of. Several thousand—I'll bet ten thousand here in Detroit."

"Followers of what?" Lynn said. She felt brave with Juvenal across the table.

August turned and looked at her for the first time as he said, "The Society of Saint Pius X, the traditionalist movement to restore Latin to the mass and sacramental worship."

He meant it too. God, Lynn thought, you don't fool

with August. It was funny Juvenal could get away with his remarks, his amused expression.

Juvenal said, "How about the Gray Army of the Holy Spirit, August? How's that doing?"

"The Gray Army of the Holy *Ghost*," August said. "We have currently over two hundred active members. Most of them, incidentally, will be out at Saint John Bosco Sunday. Did you get your invitation?"

Juvenal was looking down at the paper again. "Yeah, I did, but I don't know if I can make it."

"What's the Gray Army of the Holy Ghost?" Lynn said.

"I told Father Nestor I was sure you'll be at the dedication," August said. "You can imagine how important it is to him, his first parish."

"I'd like to—" Juvenal said.

Lynn watched him. No, he wouldn't. He didn't know how to lie and it showed.

"—but things come up around here. Sometimes Sunday's a bad day."

"I would think you'd feel obligated," August said, "a former religious giving support to a brother—"

"You'll have a lot of people, won't you?"

"Father Nestor and I both assume with your background and what you've experienced, ten years in the order—"

"Eleven," Juvenal said.

Something was going on. Lynn could feel it, something passing between them. August seemed to be quietly putting him on the spot, with even a subtle hint of blackmail.

"Eleven," August said. "How many, four years at Sao Pio Decimo." He leaned close to the table. "You think that's a coincidence? Pio Decimo, Pius the Tenth. Father Nestor said the children would ask you if you'd seen ghosts and witches—"

"I told them no ghosts, a few witches," Juvenal said. "They'd hustle guys in the back of the church."

August didn't smile. He said, "How can you dedicate eleven years of your life to God, then throw it all away?"

"I haven't thrown it away," Juvenal said. "I was into that, now I'm into something else."

"Taking care of drunks— It doesn't seem a waste to you?"

"What should I be doing?" Juvenal said.

And August said, "I don't have to tell you."

Very dramatic, almost grim. Lynn glanced at August. So serious he was weird. While Juvenal leaned on his arms and was patient. She should probably get up and leave them alone; but that seemed dumb after going to all the trouble to get here. Now in a front-row seat. If they wanted her to leave somebody would have to push her out.

It wouldn't be Juvenal—her new buddy, already feeling close to him and not knowing why. He said to her, "What did you want to know? Oh, you asked about the Gray Army of the Holy Ghost." And looked at August.

"The Gray Army is the task force corps of Outrage, our activist group," August said.

"They're the demonstrators," Juvenal said. "They wear armbands and pass out literature and get arrested. Isn't that right, August?"

August was giving Juvenal a silent, dramatic stare. "I think we should have a few words in private."

Lynn began to move, picking up her cigarettes; but Juvenal said, "Listen, I'm gonna have to get back to work, but why don't you two stay and talk?"

August got up, taking the newspaper, folding it as he said, "Father Nestor's waiting for me. I'll tell him you'll be there Sunday, all right? In fact I'll pick you up."

Juvenal shrugged and said fine. Maybe to get rid of the guy, Lynn wasn't sure. She watched August walking

away and called after him, "It was nice meeting you!"
But August didn't look back. She said to Juvenal, "You
were gonna leave me with him?"

"Why? August is fun. Don't you think so?"

"He's a spook," Lynn said. "In fact the whole thing
was spooky. What's going on Sunday?"

"A church dedication. I used to know the pastor and,
I don't know, he'd like me to be there."

"There's more to it than that," Lynn said.

Juvenal was looking at his watch. "I've got to get
going." He slid out of the booth, taking his cup.

Lynn said, "Can I talk to you later on?"

"Let's see what happens," Juvenal said, again the
mystery man.

7

In the car, August Murray's black Dodge Charger, Father Nestor said, "I should have talked to him if you're not sure."

"I didn't say I wasn't sure, I said at first he tried to get out of it. He was different," August said. "He wasn't as . . . like humble as he was the other times."

"He practiced humility. As I remember he was very humble, obedient, as we all were . . . poor, and I presume, chaste. Poverty, chastity, and obedience—now, I don't know." Father Nestor's head nodded with the motion of the car. He said then, "Oh, my, I think I have to go to the toilet."

"Why didn't you go while we were there?"

"I did. I have to go again."

August didn't say anything for a minute or so. He was thinking of a headline for a pamphlet he'd print—also use it as a news release—when he got back to the shop. *The Brother Juvenal Story.* No—

The Miracle-Working Missionary.

The Miracle Worker of the Amazon.

"I have to go bad," Father Nestor said.

In the Footsteps of Saint Francis. A modern-day Franciscan friar . . .

"Once the urge comes," Father Nestor said, "there

isn't much I can do. The doctor says a parasite in my intestine causes the dysentery. I could have it for years.''

''We'll be there in a few minutes,'' August said, moving the Charger north on Gratiot Avenue, shifting lanes in the homebound traffic, blowing his horn at cars poking along. ''Half asleep,'' August said. ''They stop off for a shot and a beer and can't see their way home. End up in a drunk tank. I don't know, I can't figure it out why he's working in a place like that. I said, 'Don't you think it's a waste?' ''

''I hope we're almost there,'' Father Nestor said.

August Murray's Zippy Printing was on Conner, across from the Detroit City Airport, within a few blocks of De La Salle, where August had attended high school, and less than a mile from Saint David, on East Outer Drive, where he had gone to grade school. August Murray was thirty-seven, had never been married, did not date girls, and had been a member of Saint David Parish all his life, except for a year and a half in the seminary. His parents had moved to Tampa, Florida. He lived alone now in the apartment over his shop, above the black-and-yellow sign that said ZIPPY PRINTING and, smaller, WHILE-U-WAIT.

August parked in back, off the alley, hurried with his ring of fifteen keys, and pointed to the lavatory as he went in through the back hall. Father Nestor walked in stiff-legged behind him.

August's own father would have walked in here and had a fit—the shop silent in half light that showed through the storefront venetian blinds. A quiet printing shop was a sin. Offset presses, A.B. Dick 360's, doing nothing. The IBM copier sitting there; the camera, the cutter and folder at the end of the worktable—the room close, smelling of ink. His father had printed parish bulletins and napkins and matchbooks and kept his accounts at the blond-wooden desk against the wall. August dropped his newspaper on the desk and turned on the electric fan that sat on the file cabinet.

With all that was happening, August wasn't going to waste his time on cocktail napkins and matchbooks.

He wished the priest would hurry up. Old priests in shiny black suits, withered necks sticking out of round Roman collars, seemed more useless than old laymen in sport shirts and straw hats. What did you do with them? Let them say six o'clock mass at a side altar somewhere—

Unless you were lucky enough to find one like Nestor and you saw the opportunity to squeeze a little more use out of him.

Father Nestor Czarnicki, OFM, fifty-two years a priest, nineteen years of it served in Santarem, Brazil, on the Amazon River. Returned with amebic dysentery and a story about a Franciscan brother who performed miracles.

Nestor Czarnicki—uncle of Greg Czarnicki, member of the Gray Army of the Holy Ghost—invited to a meeting to tell about his life as a missionary. And August stunned by what he heard (''And with the healing of the child, the manifestation of the blood; this, to me, the unmistakable sign . . .'') and the opportunity he saw before him.

Father Nestor, who said mass in a mixture of Latin and Portuguese, never in English, no, he could never do that. If he had to he would leave the order, move to France and join Archbishop Marcel Lefebvre, God's champion in returning the use of Latin to sacred rites.

''Wait,'' August had said to him. ''Talk about signs— don't you see it? You come from Seminario Sao Pio Decimo and find, already established here, the Society of Saint Pius X.''

A society with the same name whose direct purpose is to reinstitute the Latin tradition?

And the Franciscan Brother Juvenal, also returned from Sao Pio Decimo on the same plane— Wasn't that another sign?

August had to remain calm, keep himself from trying to do everything at once. Meet Juvenal, cultivate a relationship, but not bring him into the picture just yet. The plan, first, was to establish a new parish, put Nestor in as pastor, and invite Archbishop Lefebvre over to consecrate the church, the same way the Pius the Tenthers down in Texas did it.

Five months later Outrage had leased the empty Covenant Baptist Church in Almont, rechristened it Saint John Bosco, and they were on their way. A minor problem—correspondence with Lefebvre indicated it would be at least a year before he could come for the consecration. In the meantime Father Nestor might give one last grunt and expire on the toilet. So the plan was revised. Instead of consecrating the church, they would officially "dedicate it to the accepted traditions of the Catholic Faith as established by Jesus Christ, the Son of God." A series of pamphlets was run off at Zippy Printing and distributed at parish masses throughout the Archdiocese of Detroit, inviting Catholics to "Come to Saint John Bosco in Almont, the Seat of Traditional Catholic Worship." Pamphlets appeared with the titles:

WITHOUT TRADITIONS WHERE ARE WE?

WE WILL NOT ABANDON OUR TRUE FAITH.

WHY THE HOLY GHOST FLEW VATICAN II.

And August's favorite, WHY DO PRIESTS TODAY THINK THEY KNOW MORE THAN GOD?

The appeals brought them in gradually, a few dozen more traditionalists each week, until last Sunday August had estimated well over two hundred at the ten o'clock High Mass and Benediction. (Many commenting after that it'd been years since they had sung good old *Genitoris* and *Tantum Ergo*. And, boy, was it good to hear Latin again instead of those boring Protestant hymns.) They had also announced the dedication to be this coming Sunday and sent out invitations to parishioners, friends, and the press.

What August had to do now, with Father Nestor's help, was prepare a press release to be handed out *after*. "The Juvenal Story" or "The Miracle Worker"—something like that, basic information about Juvenal. Because if it worked out the way he hoped it would the newspapers would have to feature it on the front page and they'd be asking all kinds of questions.

Father Nestor—out of the lavatory, sitting across the desk from August—said, "Newspaper reporters will be there? You think so?"

"I know they will," August said, "because I'll be there and it happens that I'm news." He nodded to the paper on the desk. "I'm in there, aren't I? I staged a demonstration in court to make sure I'd be. Whatever I'm involved in is news. And what we're involved in together, specifically, what they refer to as church disunity and schism, that's news too. Reporters will be there, take my word. That's why I want to get this news release ready." August took the silver pen from his shirt pocket and released the point. "There're a few facts I don't think you told me, like where he was born, first."

"In Chicago," Father Nestor said. "You see, everyone who goes to Santarem is from the Chicago Province. Before I went, though, I served at Saint Paschal Friary in West Monroe, Louisiana, and also at Saint Joseph in Bastrop, Louisiana—"

August said, "Father, we're talking about Juvenal. His parents still live in Chicago?"

"He doesn't have parents that he knows of," Father Nestor said. "He lived in foster homes and at Our Lady of Mercy, a home for boys. You've heard of Father Kelly? He's dead now—"

"Father—" August began.

Father Nestor waved his hand at him. "All right, I

know. He was at the home—let me see—he went to work at a hospital and shortly after that he entered the order.''

''You were in Santarem a long time before he came—''

''It's pronounced Santa*reng*,'' Father Nestor said. ''Oh, yes, many years.''

''So that you helped him along, showed him the ropes maybe?''

''No, you see I was at Sao Pio Decimo and he was, most of the time he was at Convento Sao Raimundo. Or, let me think, he may have been at Convento de Nossa Senhora Nazare.''

''You knew him though.''

''Yes, I met him. And we came home together on the same flight.''

''Wait, first I want to stay down there.''

''You want to go to Santarem?''

''No—no, I want to talk about the time you met him,'' August said, ''when the miracles started, how it came about, and the first time you saw the blood.''

''Wait,'' Father Nestor said. ''I think I have to go to the toilet.''

8

Jerry said he'd close his eyes and see this guy coming right through the wall at him.

The man next to him said he saw these slimy things like lizards crawling all over the room and jumping on the bed and he'd scream and try and knock them off but they kept coming. Like lizards.

Jerry said this guy who came through the wall had a knife raised, ready to stab him with it.

Edith, Lynn's Big Sister, said, "I know, sometimes I've heard them screaming clear up on four."

Lynn stared at the wall, at the crucifix and the photograph of the room in the condemned building. It was dark outside; bright with fluorescent lighting inside, showing sticky spots and cigarette ashes on the formica.

Edith rapped her knuckles on a wet stain of coffee saying, "Well, I never had no d.t.'s, thank the Lord for that."

The Lord, on that varnished cross holding his hip-cocked pose of agony.

"Excuse me," Edith said. "Lynn, hon, you want another cup?"

Lynn's gaze came away from the crucifix. "I'll get it." She slid out of the booth, taking their cups over to the twin urns.

Something to do. She didn't need more coffee and she wasn't too keen on listening to more stories about alcoholism. She had watched television for nearly four hours after supper, on and off, looking around for Juvenal between programs. There wasn't anything to do but go to bed or sit and listen. She came back to the table with two coffees.

Jerry was saying, yeah, he used to hide them in the garage different places, even in the shrubs. That's why he was always out cutting the grass.

The man next to him said in his apartment, when he'd clean it up about once a month, he'd reach under the couch and drag out all these empty bottles.

Jerry said, "You ever reach under there and come out with a full one you forgot about? Put it on the table next to about half a fifth you got left? Man, knowing you're set for the day? Jesus, that was a good feeling."

Lynn said to Edith, setting the cups down, "I'll be back in a little bit."

"They usually don't talk that much about drinking or d.t.'s unless a new resident's asking questions, or sometimes you'll get a person who maybe wants to impress you," Juvenal said.

"I was impressed, but I got tired of it," Lynn said. She paused. "I was looking for you earlier."

"I had to go out on a call."

"This is your office?" It was exactly like the woman counselor's office she had been in this morning. In fact, from the hall, seeing the light on inside, she had thought it was the same one and thought of the telephone on the desk.

Juvenal had a phone too.

He nodded, sitting back in the chair with his pleasant expression, wearing the same red-and-blue-striped knit shirt. "I use this one if I have the duty; I can hear better if anyone starts to freak out. My room's way down the end of the hall.''

"I won't bother you,'' Lynn said, starting to turn, but giving him time to stop her.

"No, sit down. You want to ask me something, don't you?''

Lynn eased into the chair next to the desk, facing him. "Well, when you put it like that, and since I've blown my cover—''

"Your cover wasn't that red hot to begin with. Quinn already suspected you're straight.''

Lynn was surprised. "I only talked to him for a minute. The first time I saw him he came roaring into that big room that's like an auditorium on a motor scooter. Got off and gave the most fascinating talk I've ever heard.''

"He makes an entrance,'' Juvenal said. "Have you seen the fire engine? . . . It's a real old one. He gets a bunch of residents on the back end and they go for a ride downtown, ringing the bell, waving at people—it's part of the therapy, get the alcoholic out of his shell.''

"Maybe before I leave—'' Lynn said.

"You don't need to be brought out,'' Juvenal said. "You're fine.''

"Aren't you a little irritated? I mean I tell you I've come here to find out about you— But you aren't mad or anything.''

"I haven't told you anything either,'' Juvenal said. "You hear a story and you wonder about it, you and your friend Bill Hill— That reminds me. You were a baton twirler in a re*lig*ious service?''

"What were you doing, checking on me?''

"I spoke to Virginia today, so I asked about you.''

"It wasn't exactly during the service,'' Lynn said. "I twirled a little while the choir was singing, just the opening part and the close.''

"I'd like to've seen that."

"The part of the service that was the feature, Reverend Bobby Forshay'd come out and heal people."

Was Juvenal grinning a little? She wasn't sure. He said, "What do you want me to ask you, how he did it?"

"No, it was fake," Lynn said. "At least I think most of it was. I'm not sure."

It was a nice expression—not amused, but almost a smile—interested and open, glad to be talking to her. Could that be?

"Bobby might've healed some of them. You think it's possible?"

"Why not?" Juvenal said.

"Do you heal people?"

"I guess so."

"How do you do it?"

"I don't know. I mean it's not something I can explain."

"Wow," Lynn said, "this is weird, you know it? You're actually telling me—like if I had something wrong with me, a disease or something, you could cure it? Or do you say heal it?"

Juvenal hesitated, though he continued to stare at her—nice brown eyes and those long lashes—

"Is there something you're worried about?"

"Well, I'm not sure," Lynn said. "I guess I'm worried, yes; but I don't know if I should be or not."

He reached across the corner of the desk, brushed her right shoulder, the scooped neck of the loose-fitting Bob Marley shirt, and put his hand on her breast.

She couldn't believe it, feeling his hand on her, the gentle pressure of his fingers, through the bleached cotton, as they stared at each other. She thought of pulling back, with some kind of horrified expression, but realized the time to do that instinctively had already passed.

Juvenal said, "You were going to tell me you have a

lump, maybe a tumor, and if it's malignant would I do something." His hand came away. "Was it to test me or shock me?"

Lynn hesitated. "I don't know. Maybe both."

"If you're worried," Juvenal said, "take my word, your breasts are okay."

Now, instinctively, she almost said, Just okay? But in her mind it sounded dumb instead of funny; typing herself with a smartass comeback; or he might even think she was on the make. She wasn't at all, and knew he wasn't. And yet the touch hadn't been clinical either. He wasn't a doctor, he wasn't a lover—what was he?

"I don't know," Lynn said. "This's a new one I'll have to figure out."

"Figure what out?" Juvenal said.

"I plan something, it looks simple, to see if you're real or not. Then I get more confused than I was before."

"Don't try so hard," Juvenal said. He got up from the desk—striped shirt and faded jeans, white sneakers, the drunk counselor. "I'll be back."

"Where're you going?"

"I think it's Arnold. He's been having a bad time." Juvenal left.

To get away from her? Lynn hadn't heard a sound. She remembered Arnold, though, a man with a nose like a walnut, broken blood vessels in his face, his eyes barely open—she remembered him this morning groping his way into the lab, moving stiffly in sagging wet pajama pants, and the nurse calling out, "Somebody take care of Arnold!"

Lynn looked at the phone on the desk. Earlier in the evening, searching for Juvenal, she had tried the different counselors' offices, found them all locked. Now a phone was sitting within reach. Make a quick call—

She heard the sound then from down the hall, a scream,

or someone calling out, and thought of Juvenal again, curious, wondering about him, then anxious.

Lynn stepped out of the office and followed the sound down the dimly lighted hall, a man's voice wailing in agony, or fright. There was a worn-out easy chair in the hall where, they had told her, residents sat in shifts throughout the night on "heavy duty," to help anyone in detox who might begin hallucinating. But tonight Juvenal had been alone on the floor . . .

Juvenal standing next to Arnold's bed now—she could see him through the open doorway, light from the hall across the chenille cover—Arnold sitting up, his back pressed against the headboard, screaming, holding himself, trying to hide inside himself.

Juvenal moved. Past Juvenal's arm she saw Arnold's face, the man's eyes stretched open, his chin glistening with saliva. He was saying something, though she wasn't sure, that sounded like, "Don't don't don't—don't let it don't let it—" Sobbing, convulsing, as he cried out . . . then stopped as Juvenal moved in front of him and she could no longer see Arnold's face . . . stopped that suddenly and seemed to let his breath out in a moan as Juvenal sat on the edge of the bed and took Arnold's head and shoulders into his arms.

God—

Lynn could feel the chills-and-thrills on the back of her neck and down her arms, giant goosebumps. But aware and thinking at the same time, seeing her chance.

There was no sound as she turned and hurried back through the hallway to Juvenal's office, hesitated with her hand on the door, left it open—what difference did it make?—picked up the phone and dialed Bill Hill's number.

"I'm getting out of here tonight. Pick me up."

"Wait a minute," Bill Hill said. "What's wrong?"

"Nothing's wrong. I want to get out of here."

"You talked to him already?"

"I talked to him and he's real. I don't know what he is, but he's real. He *knows* things. I've done my job and now I want to leave."

"Wait, okay?" Bill Hill said. "You see him heal somebody?"

"Not exactly, but I think I know why he's here. Pick me up in front. What'll it take you, about a half hour?"

"Little more'n that, I got to get dressed," Bill Hill said. "Tell me what happened."

"Nothing happened. Well, it did, but not something you'd say is proof he heals people." She paused a moment. "I told him why I'm here."

"You *told* him—"

"He knew anyway, I could tell. He knew I wasn't an alcoholic."

"Didn't you act it out any?"

"I tried but . . . it's different. They don't act like drunks. Listen, he's not the only one. Everybody here knows something I don't. I don't fit in."

"Tell me what he said to you."

"He said lots of things. I mean in a way he did. But you look at it another way, he didn't say anything."

"Well, can you talk to him some more?"

"For what?" Lynn said. "What do you want me to do with him?"

"Just tell me what his game is, okay? What's he doing there, hiding or what?"

"It isn't something—" Lynn paused. "Look, I can usually relate to just about anybody, no matter what kind of trip they're on. You just sort of get involved and find out where their head is. But Juvenal isn't *on* any kind of trip that I know of. He isn't off somewhere or playing a role, trying to impress you, he's right here. But there's something . . . not strange, *different* about him."

"Different how?"

"It's like he's so natural he's different."

"Natural, huh?" Bill Hill didn't sound too enthused.

"He doesn't lay anything on you, any funny words or mystic-sounding bullshit you think about later, 'What was he talking about?' That's what I'm trying to say, he absolutely doesn't bullshit you or try to make you think he knows something you don't even though he *does.* Earlier today I thought he was putting a guy on, a real weird guy, a religious freak, but now I think about it—no, he was being straight with the guy. He knew *I* knew the guy was a little weird, maybe the way I rolled my eyes or something, but he accepted the guy. I mean this guy came across as a really serious asshole of the worst kind. You could see Juvenal didn't agree with the guy, but he seemed to be interested in him as a *person* and kidded with him. That's another thing; he doesn't seem to take serious things serious."

"He doesn't, huh?"

"Only *one* time Juvie tried to bullshit the guy a little, you could see he didn't know how—"

"About what?"

"Listen, I've got to get off the phone. Pick me up in forty minutes, okay? And get a bottle of Spumante—"

9

Lynn waited about ten minutes. When Juvenal didn't come back she got up and walked down the hall again, past the empty chair.

There was the sound of someone snoring now, a soft, faint sound; it made her aware of how quiet it was on the floor. People sleeping . . . people down on the second floor having coffee, watching television . . . she wondered if she should say good-bye to Edith and some of the others. If she did, she would have to make up a story, a crisis at home, or she couldn't take the program or she was going nuts cooped up here and they'd plead with her to sit down and talk, or talk to Juvie or Father Quinn. She wouldn't go down to two, she'd stay up here. She didn't have anything to pack—

Arnold's door was still open. Juvenal wasn't in the room.

Lynn stood in the opening, then moved aside to let the light from the hallway fall across the bed. Arnold was lying on his back, eyes closed, hands relaxed on the light chenille spread covering him. She could hear Arnold inhaling gently and letting his breath out in a wheeze that was not quite a snore. But no Juvenal. He could have gone to get Arnold a sleeping pill—no, Edith said they rarely use them here, or tranquilizers—but he could have gone to get him *some*thing. She began to turn away, still looking at Arnold, then turned back again and very carefully, quietly, approached the bed, moving aside, staying out of the light, so she could see Arnold's face clearly. There was something on his cheek, something dark. Lynn stooped, then went to one knee next to the bed, looking at the dark streak that crossed from Arnold's cheekbone to the corner of his mouth. Her hand went to the bed lamp, felt beneath the shade and found the button. Looking at Arnold she turned the lamp on—saw the mark on his face become red in the light, a smudge of something red, wiped and streaked; saw the stains on the pillow, blood red, and thought of Virginia, Bill Hill telling about the traces of blood on Virginia's face—and snapped off the lamp. She knelt there a moment, her hands on the edge of Arnold's bed, as though in prayer.

Two doors away a light was on in the lab. No one was inside. Lynn moved past the lab and several rooms, looking at closed doors, to the end of the hall where the carpeted floor joined a short, perpendicular hallway with a door at each end. The overhead light was dim, not more than 75 watts, but she could make out the metal nameplate on the door to the left, JUVENAL—hesitant now approaching the door, afraid. She said to herself, Afraid of what? He's nice. He's a very nice guy. She knocked lightly on the door—God, and saw the mark, the stain on the knob, and almost drew back. The door was open several inches. She knocked again, holding back, tapping lightly the way she would enter a sickroom and said, "Juvenal?"

Silence.

Lynn pushed the door open. She stood looking in at a desk and soft light reflecting on French doors that were partly open and led to a rooftop porch. The light came from a reading lamp next to a dark leather couch. There were bookshelves to the ceiling and grass mats on the floor, a crucifix over the desk.

She could hear running water.

"Juvenal?"

The sound of the water stopped. Lynn walked into the room. To the right was a short hallway. She waited; but she was curious and anxious again, with the same feeling she had experienced before, wanting to know what he was doing. She told herself he was good and wouldn't hurt her, he *healed* people—

She stepped into the hallway. The light was on in the bathroom, on the left, and she glanced in. There were red stains on the rim of the basin, traces of red not washed into the drain.

She said again, "Juvenal?"

His voice came from the bedroom, tired, a quiet sound. "I'm in here."

"Can I come in?"

There was a silence.

"If you want to."

Lynn walked into the bedroom.

He stood in white undershorts by a dresser, his chest and legs bare. He stood on a white towel, his feet bare.

Lynn said, "Oh, my God—"

She saw his mild expression, his eyes. She saw his hands raised at his sides, palms up, as if holding small pools of blood.

She saw the crucifix on the wall in the coffee shop.

She saw the blood on his hands. She saw the blood oozing out of his left side, staining the waistband of his shorts. She saw the blood on his bare feet, red gouge marks on his insteps, the blood trickling to the towel.

She saw the crucifix again, the agonized figure of Christ on the cross.

She saw Juvenal standing in his bedroom, bleeding from the same five wounds.

10

On Friday Greg Czarnicki, member of the Gray Army of the Holy Ghost and Father Nestor's nephew, said to August, "Wait a minute. How many people you think ever heard of it?"

August said, "Everybody's heard of it one time or another. Padre Pio—he just died. Theresa Neumann, they've been some very famous ones."

"You've got Padre Pio and Theresa Neumann, but I'm saying outside of Catholics who ever heard of them?" Greg said.

"Padre Pio got five thousand letters a week," August said. "They lined up, you had to wait two months to go to confession to him."

"Yeah, devout people," Greg said. "But how many even Catholics are really devout?"

"Saint Francis of Assisi," August said.

"Okay, Saint Francis," Greg said, "but how many people know he had it?"

"Maybe you're right," August said.

"How do you know Juvie's even gonna get it?"

"We don't," August said, "but you're right. Maybe I've been assuming too much. Greg? . . . Thanks." August sat down at his father's desk in the print shop and wrote a pamphlet that would be handed out Sunday in the event everything worked the way he hoped it would. The pamphlet was entitled:

STIGMATA
The Wounds of Christ Crucified . . .
The Marks of Sainthood!

And told the reader:

> The stigmata is a phenomenon observed in a number of Christian saints and mystics for which there is no *natural* explanation. Therefore it is assumed the stigmata is of supernatural origin or inspiration. It consists of the appearance, on the body of a living person, of wounds that correspond to our Lord Jesus Christ's wounds on the cross—the nail wounds in his hands and feet and the wound from the Roman soldier's spear thrust into His side.

321 KNOWN STIGMATISTS

A study conducted by Dr. A. Imbert-Gourbeyre (*La Stigmasation,* 2 v. Clermont-Ferrand, 1894–95; 2nd edition, 1908) contains the names of 321 people who have manifested the stigmata since the time of St. Francis of Assisi (1181–1226), the Church's first recorded stigmatist. Pope Pius XI has stated that the stigmata of St. Francis is an historical fact proved by irrefutable testimonies. The list includes a number of the more recent stigmatists who have been written about, such as: Catherine Emmerich of Muenster, Germany (1774–1824), Mary von Moerl of Kaltern, Tyrol (1812–1868), Louise Lateau of Bois de Haine, France (1850–1883), St. Gemma Galgani of Lucca, Italy (1878–1903).

BLED FROM HER EYES

One of our most prominent stigmatists was Theresa

Neumann of Konnersreuth, Germany, born on Good Friday, April 8, 1898. Her first stigmatization appeared on Good Friday, April 2, 1926, when her eyes began to bleed profusely, a phenomenon that would occur whenever she meditated on Christ's suffering. Theresa Neumann's stigmata brought pilgrims from all over the world. It was seen by thousands of people and subject to intensive investigation. She died in 1962 after virtually living on no other nourishment than Holy Communion.

PADRE PIO—MOST FAMOUS OF ALL

There is no question that the most celebrated stigmatist of any time is Padre Pio, the Capuchin monk of San Giovanni Rotondo in southern Italy, who received the stigmata one day in September 1918, three days after the feast of the stigmata of St. Francis. While at prayer in the chapel of Maria delle Grazie, he was found in a faint, blood pouring from his five wounds. He experienced fresh bleeding every day of his life for the next 50 years.

Over 100 biographies have been written about Padre Pio, describing his wounds, the miracles performed through his intercession, and offering medically attested evidence that his stigmata was not a natural phenomenon.

ODOR OF VIOLETS

Drs. Festa and Romanelli, who examined Padre Pio, stated that all five wounds had a characteristic odor of violets and that the one in the saintly man's side was in the form of a cross seven centimeters in length. Their report could offer no explanation of the cause of the lesions nor of their refusal to heal.

MIRACLES

Padre Pio was famous for performing miracles, curing

the sick and infirm, and for his gift of "bilocation," being able to be in two places at once. There are accounts of his actually appearing to soldiers during World War II and saving them from death, while he remained in the monastery at San Giovanni Rotondo.

"He received 5,000 letters a week and about 1,500,000 visitors a year. (*National Review,* Oct. 22, 1968) There is a library full of testimony by sane, well-educated, unprejudiced people to the effect that he was really gifted with an odor of sanctity, that he was often reported in two places at the same time, and that he continually, but especially in the confessional, displayed intimate knowledge of the secret thoughts, sins, prayers, temptations and devotional lives of the people he spoke to. . . . He died September 23, 1968, having carried the open wounds of the stigmata longer than anyone else in history; for 50 years he had not taken a step without the slow, painful gait of a crippled man. When they wanted to call a doctor he said, 'Be good fellows, don't call anybody. Those whom I ought to call, I have already called.' "

AND NOW . . .
A decade has passed since anyone has been blessed with the mystical gift of the stigmata . . . a period of time in which Holy Mother Church has been besieged and buffeted by false doctrines, liberal attempts to make the bastion of our Faith a lukewarm, lackadaisical, Protestant-like symbol of "all things to all men."

One wonders if it is not now time for the stigmata to appear again on a person of devotion and dedication . . . a person bearing the Marks of Faith, the Symbols of Sanctity, who would stand before us as a present-day St. Francis . . . to lead us 'round the quicksand of heresy and reestablish, reaffirm the traditional

teaching ministry of the Church of Jesus Christ and His
Apostles. We await the Sign crying:

> **O**rganization
> **U**nifying
> **T**raditional
> **R**ites
> **A**s
> **G**od
> **E**xpects
> **!!!**

August read the pamphlet to Greg Czarnicki.

Greg said, "How come you don't mention Juvie?"

"Because nobody knows about him yet." August said.
"Don't you see what I'm doing? I'm setting it up, like
saying we need a symbol, a sign, and there he is. Can
you imagine the impact? I still can't believe it—no, I
don't mean that, I don't want to infer a lack of faith. But
it gives me the chills thinking about it. Like there's no
question God has His hand on me and is using me. Do
you feel it?"

Greg nodded, yes, he did. He would have felt it more,
though, if August said "us" instead of "me." Like
something miraculous was happening to August.

11

"I hate to say it," Lynn said, "but the last time I was in church was at Uni-Faith in Dalton. No, I take that back, I went with Doug when his sister got married in Fort Worth. But you know what I did today? I bought a dress. And I haven't owned a dress I bet since I was a little girl, a regular *dress*. At first I thought it was a housedress because it's just a print, you know. But, God, it was eighty dollars because it's a Diane Von Furstenburg." Lynn paused. "I guess it's kind of cute really."

The phone rang inside, sounding far away.

Lynn and Bill Hill were on the balcony, outside but private on the second floor, behind the railing and the hanging plants. Lynn didn't move, slumped low in a red canvas chair, bare legs stretched out. Bill Hill was on the matching red chaise looking down the quiet twilight fairway, seeing himself loft an approach to number seventeen that dropped within inches of the cup. He looked over at Lynn.

"You don't have the phone with you."

"Shit," Lynn said. She drew her legs under her, but didn't get up. "No, I quit carrying it around from room to room. Two days, I've pretty near forgotten all about the business."

"How do you know it's business?"

"Who's gonna call me eight o'clock Saturday night? The guys're out with their wives. It's Artie, from the Coast."

The phone continued to ring.

"I asked you one time, you never told me. How come all those guys sound like they're from New York?"

"Like gangsters talk in the movies," Bill Hill said. "I don't know, I guess it's supposed to impress you. . . . You gonna answer it?"

Lynn got up, barefoot in white shorts and a white shirt hanging out hiding the shorts, looking like a little girl, scrubbed clean and not wearing her eyelashes. She took her time going inside, hoping the phone would stop ringing.

Bill Hill was always nice to Lynn. He liked her a lot. There was a time, after finding her divorced and living in Detroit—couple of old buddies up here six hundred miles from home—he'd thought about making the moves to get her in bed. But when he pictured himself doing it, he knew he'd be self-conscious and both of them would probably laugh. That was it, they were buddies—even with a twenty-year difference in their ages—they told each other things and confided; they were like kin.

She had certainly been in a state Thursday night, come running out of the Sacred Heart Center, jumped in the car saying, "God, you're not gonna believe it," and hadn't told him clearly, in words that made sense, until they were out on the Chrysler Freeway and past the Ford interchange, midway through Detroit going north.

He had tried to keep his eyes on the road and not ask questions, trying also to picture what she was telling him, finally saying, "You mean *nails* were in him?" And Lynn saying, "No, *wounds* like from nails and a cut in his side like he'd been stabbed."

"Jesus."

"Yes, *Jesus*," Lynn said. "Standing there like him.

Honest to God, if he had a beard—you know like the pictures you see of him, the brown hair? His hair's the same color.''

"What did he say?"

"Nothing. He just looked at me."

"Was he in pain?"

"No, I don't think so. He seemed, like he was sad. I don't know, he was just—quiet."

"And he didn't say anything."

"No. Well, yes, he did. He said my name, I remember now hearing it as I ran out. God, why'd I do that?"

"I can understand," Bill Hill said.

"He didn't yell it out I remember, going out, I heard him say it. 'Lynn?' " She tried it again—" 'Lynn?' "— trying to get the right tone.

"You think he wanted you to help him?"

"*Help* him? Help him what, put Band-Aids on? He had the same wounds as Jesus on the cross and he hadn't been crucified and he didn't do it himself. There weren't any nails or a knife or anything; he wasn't showing it off, but—well, yes he was too—he was showing it to me." Lynn was silent. "You think he did want me to help him? God, and I ran out; turned and ran like a little kid."

"He must know what to do," Bill Hill said, "if he had it before."

"But why'd he show it to me?"

Bill Hill said, "Maybe the people there know and he felt it didn't matter, one more. Remember my telling you I thought they were keeping him hidden? Very friendly and helpful, except they didn't tell you a thing. If a man wanted to remain anonymous that'd be the place, wouldn't it?"

"But people leave there," Lynn said. "They'd tell; somebody would."

"I mean the staff," Bill Hill said. "I can't imagine that priest not knowing."

"Father Quinn," Lynn said, thoughtful. "I suppose the doctor—"

Bill Hill said, "Did you happen to notice his hands before? I mean when you were talking to him earlier?"

Lynn thought about it, picturing him in the coffee shop, then in the office, seeing his hand reaching for her breast. She hadn't told Bill Hill about that part and didn't think she would.

"I didn't notice anything special. Like you mean if he had scars?"

"I think he'd have to," Bill Hill said. "If a wound keeps opening up there's got to be a scar. Wouldn't you think?"

"I don't know. If it's a miracle why does there have to be anything natural about it?"

"Who says it's a miracle?"

"That's right," Lynn said, "you see people every day walking around with crucifixion wounds."

There had been a lot to think about in the dark interior of Bill Hill's Monte Carlo, heading out the Chrysler Freeway that night, the radio off, Lynn, for the first time not skipping around on the AM-FM to see if her records were getting any play. No, it was quiet, and the fluorescent glow of light beneath the overpasses added to the feeling—something happening they couldn't explain no matter how hard they thought about it. Juvenal's blood on Virginia's face and on the man with d.t.'s. Like it happened to him when he was healing somebody . . . maybe when he was in an emotional state, feeling compassion or something so intensely he began to bleed?

Lynn asked Bill Hill if he'd ever heard of anybody having it before. He said yes, he'd heard of it but had never read much about it or knew of anyone who'd had it lately. He believed it was something a long time ago saints used to get.

"God, saints," Lynn had said.

"I guess not all saints," Bill Hill had said, "just some."

Lynn came out on the balcony and sank into the canvas chair.

"Hey, thanks."

Bill Hill had filled her wine glass and made himself a fresh vodka and bitter lemon. He sat on the chaise with his white loafers crossed, the crease in his yellow slacks straight and sharp up to the lump of a bony knee, then on to the bulge of his body shirt that was like blue-flowered wallpaper, three buttons undone to show his silver chain and *Thank You, Jesus* medallion that his former wife, Barbararose, had given him years ago, way before neck ornaments for men became popular. He liked the feel of it there and sometimes liked to hook two fingers over the medallion and hang onto it. Maybe for security, though Bill Hill usually didn't analyze his moves or try to interpret his body language. He believed in Almighty God and His Only Begotten Son Jesus Christ, but did not believe in most traditional forms of worship or fundamental methods of propagating the faith. Not since his Uni-Faith days. It had been great stuff . . .

The World's Tallest Illuminated Cross of Jesus, 117 feet high . . . the Chapel in the Pines, the Pilgrims' Rest Cafeteria and Gift Shop, where they sold Heavenly Hash candy, ten-inch battery-operated replicas of the World's Tallest Illuminated Cross of Jesus, WTICOJ T-shirts . . . There were college-girl hostesses, fresh young things direct from the Florida campus at Gainesville, three state-champion baton twirlers including fabulous Lynn Marie Faulkner of Miami Beach, who had twirled in five Orange Bowl pageants before she was eighteen . . . And for the main attraction there was the Reverend Bobby Forshay, who would appear from way off coming down out of the piny woods like a 1960s John the Baptist. Bobby Forshay would mount the stage of the amphitheater in his raggedy jeans and polyester wolfskin sleeveless jacket and say, "Hi. I was up yonder talking to my old buddy Jesus. And you know what he told me? . . ." Bobby Forshay would preach and then he would invite the sick and the cripples to come up with their crutches and walkers and faith in their hearts and let him lay his hands on them and, as an instrument of the Lord, heal their infirmities. He healed a bunch of them . . .

Bill Hill's ex-wife, Barbararose, who was a hard-shell Baptist out of Nashville, where there were 686 different Fundamentalist churches, had called the whole Uni-Faith setup "a mockery in the eyes of God." (Where did people find those special words for talking about religion? *Mockery.*) "You call yourself a born-again Christian," Barbararose had said, "asking people to reverence a ten-story hunk of wood and a Bible school dropout who can no more heal'n I can."

"It's the end result that counts," Bill Hill had said. "How it makes people feel."

Barbararose said, "Do you know what the Lord thinks about all this?"

"He told you but He hasn't told me yet," Bill Hill said.

Barbararose said He would call it an abomination unto His name. For thou shalt not make unto thee any graven images, etc.

Bill Hill said to his wife, "You know why Baptists never fuck standing up, Barbararose? They don't want God to think they're dancing."

Barbararose had left him, taking along little Bill, Jr., eventually got a divorce and was now married to a fruit shipper down in Stuart, Florida. Fine. (Little Bill, Jr., now a teen-ager, visited summers and they'd take off for a month in the latest r.v. equipment.)

As for getting back in the religion business—well, there

were boys who still did all right with the old methods. Billy Graham filled the Astrodome and Oral Roberts had a university going for him and an AP top-twenty basketball club. Rex Humbard was still on TV Sunday morning and had his Cathedral of Tomorrow in Akron, Ohio. But those boys had become established over the years and worked hard to keep up their ratings.

No, there was another way to sell God and His blessings and he'd give Lynn a hint the next time she shook her head and said Juvenal wasn't salable or wasn't the kind you could use in a religious show. He'd say, "What did David Frost sell those Nixon interviews for?" She'd say what? Or she'd say she didn't know. He'd say, "Something like six million, that's what. You see it?" She'd say no. He'd say, "Sell the package and get out, that's how you do it." That's all he'd tell her today and only if she asked. Bill Hill wasn't sure yet how to go about it; but it was an idea that felt good, fooling with in his mind, one of those ideas you think of and say, "Of course. How else would you do it?"

Lynn said, "It was Artie. I told you. He's taking the red eye and'll be here in the morning. *Has* to see me."

"I thought you quit."

"I did, sort of. But I've got to give him my records and things."

"Wait a minute," Bill Hill said, "tomorrow's Sunday."

"He says he's got a presentation first thing Monday and if it doesn't come off right it's my fault."

"Well, tough. You told him, what, four days ago—"

"I know, but at least I've got to pick him up and, you know, get him squared away. He comes here, he's lost."

Bill Hill was sitting up straighter, frowning. "All you've been talking about is going up to Almont tomorrow. You're dying to see Juvenal—see what's going on with this weird guy and his Gray Ghosts—"

"I'm gonna be there. We're going, right. But I've got to meet Artie first, that's all. I'm *defi*nitely gonna be there. I have to, at least I have to apologize for running off, God, like I was scared of him. He must think I'm awful."

Bill Hill was shaking his head now. "You witnessed something few living persons have ever seen. You saw a miracle with your own eyes, and now you tell me these rock and roll records you have to give Artie are more important."

"The *busi*ness records," Lynn said. "I'm not giving him record records. Look, it starts at eleven, Saint John Bosco in Almont. I got a road map—I've got a new dress, haven't I?—I know exactly how to get there and I'm going, *we're* going. But I've got to see Artie first."

"I'll pick you up," Bill Hill said.

"Fine."

"Ten o'clock."

"Fine. Only, just in case I'm not back you go ahead and I'll meet you there."

Bill Hill was staring at her, hard. "You're afraid to see him, aren't you?"

"I'm not afraid, and I'm gonna be there," Lynn said. "Maybe I'm a little nervous, that's all."

"What're you gonna say to him?"

"I don't know—how are you? What do you say? I'm gonna apologize, ask if I can come and talk to him sometime. . . . What do you keep looking at me like that for?"

"I'm concerned about you," Bill Hill said. "You feel all right?"

"I feel fine."

"There's something about you that's different."

"Well, what do you expect? I just got out of an alcohol treatment center."

That was better.

He didn't want to see her tighten up and lose her sense of values, get too serious. He needed Lynn with him all the way if he was going to make his million dollars.

12

August Murray planned the dedication ceremony around Father Nestor's contaminated bowel. He knew the old man would never last two hours away from a toilet, so he planned it: procession, Solemn High Mass, break; second procession, Benediction, impromptu announcement and . . . whatever happened after that.

Following the break, Greg Czarnicki would remain outside. He wanted to be sure to tell Greg to have his camera with him at all times.

Bill Hill waited in front of Lynn's apartment until almost eleven; gave up, irritated, got lost on the way to Almont, and didn't arrive at Saint John Bosco until the second procession was moving up the walk to the church. Bill Hill didn't know he had missed the first procession, mass, and Father Nestor's halting sermon on the true spirituality of the Latin tradition. He thought the show was just beginning, and in a way he was right.

He recognized Juvenal, thinking at first he was dressed as a priest. No, more like a tall altar boy in his cassock and surplice, showing about six inches of tan cotton pants and white sneakers below the hem of the black gown. Juvenal carried a cross straight up in front of him, like a staff with a crucifix mounted on top. Behind him came

two real altar boys, about eleven or twelve, one of them
swinging a silver thing of incense—a nice touch, Bill Hill
thought, the sound of the canister swinging on thin
chains—then another guy about Juvenal's age in black
cassock and white surplice (August Murray) and then an
old priest in gold vestments flicking holy water out of
what looked like a flashlight—flicking it at the men in
white shirts and gray armbands who lined both sides of
the walk and were holding lighted candles.

Bill Hill hung back until the Gray Ghosts, or whatever
Lynn said they were called, fell in behind the priest; he
followed them into the church.

The *Detroit Free Press* had sent a writer by the name
of Kathy Worthington, twenty-nine—eight years on
murders, drug busts, city politics, fish with mercury and
milk laced with PBB—to cover the Saint John Bosco
dedication. She didn't ask why; she had covered August
Murray activities before and knew something at least
worthy of page 3, local news, could happen.

The paper had not assigned a photographer—they had
several shots of August Murray on file, both wild-eyed
and composed—and Kathy didn't see anyone from the
News or any of the television stations; which was fine.
She wouldn't have to stand around with them being
cynical. So this is where the action is, huh? Four and a
half million people either doing something or getting
ready to on a summer morning in August . . . while here
at Almont, at the dedication of Saint John Bosco . . . and
tie it in with Tremors in the Church of Rome , . .
Catholic, universal, the French Archbishop Lefebvre's
traditionalist movement—"This attitude of the Vatican
against us is not come from the Holy Ghost"—and you
have August Murray's white-shirted ghosts . . . bring
August into the story, grim defender of right-wing causes
. . . though she didn't see how he could swing very

militantly today and get busted for anything. August among his own kind: play it straight and hope that at least he'd insult the pope and call him a Communist.

Kathy Worthington's note pad remained in her canvas bag while she sat through her first mass since graduating from Immaculata High School. So far, what did you write about a mass said by an old priest who sprinkled his Latin with Portuguese? Even if Rome found out, would they give a shit?

Lynn was only about ten minutes behind Bill Hill once she was able to shake Artie loose, trying to be nice, then raising her voice and telling him no, definitely, she would *not* help him with his presentation or discuss any part of the business with him for two weeks; she was on her vacation, and if he didn't like it he could get somebody else; she had to go, she was late for church. Artie said, "You going to *church?* Who's getting married?"

She arrived to see all the cars parked along the gravel road in front of the typical white frame basic church she had seen on county roads all her life, feeling they were the same dusty cars and pickups, the same people attending—just like when she was little and would hang around outside with her friends until they heard the organ playing and the people solemnly joining in the first hymn. Lynn parked and walked down the line of cars in her blue-green eighty-dollar print, a little awkward in heels after years of sandals and wedges—it was the gravel, and wanting to hurry but still look neat and fresh when she entered.

The organ sounded like an accordion, tinny, the notes dull, repetitive. The words were different though.

"Tan-tum air-go-oh, sac-ra-meh-en-tum . . ." Mournful, a slow chant.

"Vay-nay-ray-mur cher-nu-ee-ee . . ."

She paused on the steps before the open doorway,

looking over to see a yellow school bus, *Lapeer County Schools*, pulling up to the house or rectory next door. A young guy in a choir or altar boy outfit stood in the drive with both hands raised, guiding the bus toward him past a line of parked cars. The door opened, a little boy wearing a baseball cap jumped out of the bus, and a voice called to him to wait.

Lynn didn't know if this was mass or what. She couldn't remember if she'd ever heard Latin before. The church was packed. A line of men in white shirts and gray armbands, holding lighted candles, extended up both sides of the middle aisle. The priest on the altar in gold vestments— She saw Juvenal then, the tallest altar boy up there, and August Murray, also in an altar boy outfit.

"Sol-us hon-on-or, vir-tus quo-oh-quay . . ."

The song was so sad; she wondered what it was about—looking around for Bill Hill now, her eyes seeking color.

"No-vo say-dat rit-too-ee . . ."

The congregation didn't appear much different than any other. They could be Baptist, Pentecostal, Church of God . . . the guys with the armbands, she decided, must be the Gray Army of the Holy Ghost. Fundamentalists didn't have anything like that. She wasn't even sure if they had a Holy Ghost.

"Gen-ee-tor-re-is, gen-ee-toh-oh-quay . . ."

Everybody singing and they weren't even reading it from hymnbooks. They actually knew the words.

Juvenal was facing the congregation, he and August Murray flanking the old priest, maybe holding him up. Juvenal moved aside and Lynn had the feeling he was looking at her, past all the heads and hats, picking her out where she stood in the back of the church. Smiling? Lynn wasn't sure if he was smiling at her—actually, she wasn't sure if he was smiling at all—a boyish face up there beyond all the hats.

Yes, *hats*—it dawned on her that all the women seemed to be wearing summer straws or little hats with veils she hadn't seen in years, or scarves over their heads, all of them . . . except the blonde in the last pew, just a little over from Lynn, a girl about her own age with long, straight blond hair, green shirtdress, and canvas bag.

Something something *"doe-que-men-tum,"* something else and *"la-ouw-da-ah-tsi-oh—"* And then a sustained *"Ah-men."* There was a long silence. She couldn't see what they were doing up there. Then everyone knelt down and Lynn felt exposed, the only one standing.

She saw Bill Hill, squeezed in at the end of a pew over on the far left, wearing his yellow outfit two days in a row. Black hair slicked down in place—she was pretty sure he used Grecian Formula. He looked out of place, though not because he claimed to be a Fundamentalist. He looked too studied-slick to be among the Latin-lovers.

A little altar boy was swinging something silver on a chain, thin wisps of smoke rising. Lynn realized it was incense—they actually used it in their religious ceremony. There was a faint odor, too, but it wasn't the sweet smell of incense in dark rooms with cool jazz playing. The priest turned to the congregation, raising a gold statue that was like an arty sunburst with a little round window in the center and something white showing through the glass. Bells rang several times. There was a hush inside the church, not a sound. The members of the Gray Army were down on one knee. It was moody, very dramatic, the incense, the thin little sound of the bells, the gold sunburst raised high. Bill Hill was half sitting, half kneeling, watching, not moving a muscle—the expert on God, religion, and church administration. Lynn watched him begin to turn, looking around with his head raised. She waited. When he saw her, finally, she gave him a motion to come on back. The priest was saying, in English, "The Divine Praises . . . Blessed be God."

And everyone in the church said, "Blessed be God."

"Blessed be His holy name."

Everybody: "Blessed be His holy name."

She wanted to ask him what was going on and if she'd
missed anything. Bill Hill was coming down the side aisle
now—heads turning to watch him as they answered,
"Blessed be Jesus Christ, true God and true man." Lynn
waited as he crossed the back of the church.

"Blessed be His most sacred heart."

She stage-whispered, "You see him? Juvenal?"

Bill Hill nodded, reaching her. "I think he saw me,
too, but I'm not sure."

"What's going on?"

"How should I know?" Bill Hill took her arm. "Let's
go out and grab a smoke."

Lynn hesitated, the little girl again. Was it all right?
She wasn't going to have much choice the way he was
pulling her. She said, "You should quit if you have to
leave church to have one."

He said, "Come on," starting for the vestibule,
sunlight showing in the open doorway.

The priest was saying, "Blessed be Jesus in the most
holy sacrament of the altar."

The congregation said it again.

The priest began, "Blessed be the name of Mary—"

"Blessed be the name of Mary, virgin and mother,"
the congregation said.

There was silence.

Then another voice said, "Blessed be her holy and
immaculate conception."

As the congregation repeated the words, Bill Hill
stopped to look over his shoulder at the altar.

The priest was walking stiff-legged yet hurrying to
leave the altar. For a moment Juvenal stood watching. He
went after the old priest then, close behind him as they
went through the door into the sacristy. The other adult

altar boy, August Murray, glanced after them, saying,
"Blessed be Saint Joseph, her most chaste spouse."

Bill Hill felt Lynn's hands on his arm.

"Blessed be Saint Joseph, her most chaste spouse."

He turned back to go out with her, feeling her close.
But she didn't move and he bumped against her, saying,
"What's the matter?" as he saw her expression.

"Blessed be God, His angels and His saints."

"Blessed be God, His angels and His saints."

Silence.

Lynn stood rigid, facing the vestibule.

The sunny area between the inner and outer doors of
the church seemed to be full of children. Children on
crutches, children with metal leg braces, children wearing
padded helmets, children in wheelchairs . . .

13

Father Nestor had said yes, he saw it with his own eyes, the healing of the crippled boy.

"How was he crippled?" August had asked.

"His spine was deformed. The little boy used crutches and dragged his legs. It was very difficult for him."

"Then Juvenal touched him?"

"The boy was in the road where other children were playing. Juvenal was walking by them, ahead of Brother Carlos and I. He looked at the boy and then stopped. The boy looked at Juvenal. Something passed between them; or it might have, I don't know. The boy hobbled over to Juvenal—yes, and then he touched him, dropped to his knees, and held the boy against him. The boy seemed to be taller, his crutches fell—"

"The boy was happy, smiling?"

"I don't remember. I believe he was . . . stunned, very surprised. He looked down at his legs—"

"He ran off then?"

"He walked a few feet away, then in circles, looking down at his legs."

"What about the other children—was it at the same time, the others?"

"There was a little girl with tumors on her body, very ugly sores. He took her into his arms also."

"And they disappeared, the tumors?"

"No, it was not like that. But the next day they were talking about her in the village, everyone very excited. The doctor examined her, there was nothing, no tumors on her, not even scars, and he questioned if it was the same little girl."

"What about other children?"

"I'm not sure. Perhaps."

"Did he restore anyone's sight?"

"Yes, a young man. He left the village and went to Santarem and was injured very severely in a barroom fight and died soon after. This is what they say, I have no proof of it."

"I thought it was just children."

"No, I told you, the two children I know of and a few others, a very old woman I believe with tuberculosis."

"An old *woman?*"

"Yes, I remember some of the people saying why would he waste this gift on an old woman who was worth nothing."

August Murray had been thinking the same thing. "How many did he heal?"

"I don't know. Perhaps seven or eight."

"Why didn't he heal more?"

Father Nestor seemed to smile. He said, "Yes, send him to the hospital, uh? Heal everybody. But they brought him to Convento Sao Raimundo, where he stayed until he was sent home."

"That's the part I don't understand—keeping him hidden. Why?"

"You talk to him, ask him."

"Not yet," August Murray had said. "If I talk about it and seem too interested—well, he might not agree with our way of doing things. What I like best," August had said, at that time, months before, beginning to form his plan, "is the part about the children."

August could picture the brown-skinned little boy dropping his crutches and would see him, very clearly, running through a jungle junkyard village of old adobe and rusting Coca-Cola signs, the boy shouting excitedly and with dogs chasing after him in the muddy street. A cute little Walt Disney native boy. On the screen or in advertising they said kids and dogs were the number-one attention getters and emotional motivators, right? Sex also, some half-naked woman. Well, there was no place for dogs or women in August Murray's plan. But kids— yes, kids could do it. Kids could put them on the front page of every newspaper in the country. The right kids at the right time. And, if it worked.

But if it worked down on the Amazon, why not assume it would work here? It would be the same person involved. It would be a setup and he would be taken completely by surprise, if the timing was right. But still the same person, so why wouldn't it work?

If it didn't, well, it could still get press.

14

August Murray's favorites were Scott Lenahan, eight, with cerebral palsy, who had been last year's Torch Drive poster boy; a cute little girl by the name of Betty Davis, nine, blind since birth; and Kenny Melkowski, also nine, who had spinal meningitis.

There was another kid August had liked at first, a good-looking kid named Richie Baker, age ten, who wore a Detroit Tigers baseball cap all the time. But Richie's ailment wasn't acceptably visual. He had acute lymphocytic leukemia and when he took off his baseball cap he was completely bald.

August told Greg Czarnicki to get candid shots of the kids *before*—you know, like before and after—coming off the bus; and try to maneuver them so that Scotty, Betty, and Kenny would go up the aisle first, right after the Divine Praises—though any of the dozen kids August had rounded up would probably work okay: unfortunate little kids who belonged to friends of friends . . .

(Why had God done that to these nice Catholic kids?)

. . . and had been invited to the Saint John Bosco Dedication Day Picnic following the special blessing by Father Nestor.

(So their suffering could be used for a greater good? August decided that must be the reason.)

The priest's unscheduled trip to the toilet, Juvenal running after him, had given August a sinking feeling, but only for a moment. He'd picked up the Divine Praises, finished them . . . saw Greg in the back of the church with the kids and some of the parents, Greg waiting for the cue . . . saw Juvenal coming back on the altar, Juvenal out of it just long enough and completely unaware . . . and August felt both relief and excitement, more certain than ever God was helping him.

He said to the congregation, at least 250 packed into the little church, "Father Nestor will be right back and we'll proceed with the dedication. While we have a moment though, I'd like to take this opportunity to introduce you to a very remarkable man who's dedicated a good part of his life to the foreign missions, having served down in the jungles of Brazil on the Amazon River—"

Juvenal was staring down the main aisle, past the Gray Army to the vestibule.

"—and let him say a few words to us about his experiences in witnessing God's mercy and miraculous blessing on those less fortunate than we are."

Lynn saw Juvenal's expression.

She had turned her back to the children and stood rigid, feeling them behind her, watching Juvenal now, knowing what August Murray was doing. Juvenal knew it too; of course he would. His expression seemed composed, almost bland, but with a dreamy hint of something she had seen before, a look of sadness, resignation. She wanted to be with him, help him. She wanted to stop August, shut him up. She wanted to turn around and the children would be gone.

There was the sound of a camera shutter, a repeated sound, buzz and click. Greg Czarnicki, the altar boy she had seen outside by the bus, was backing past her, a Minolta pressed to his face, aimed at the children.

"I'm going to ask our special little guests to come

forward,'' August said, arms raised high, beckoning, ''and receive the blessing of our good friend Juvenal, who has demonstrated his compassion and love of children in ways that are truly miraculous.''

The girl with the long blond hair and green dress, in the last pew, was looking around now at the children.

The two lines of the Gray Army made a half turn to face each other across the middle aisle, like a guard of honor.

Greg Czarnicki, backing up the aisle, clicked the shutter of his Minolta and the children came in their clean Sunday clothes, in their braces and on crutches, the little blind girl holding onto a wheelchair, a few with no visible signs of disease or prosthesis—parents remaining behind— the children following Greg as if drawn by his camera.

Bill Hill said, ''Jesus Christ,'' awed, close to Lynn.

She saw the blond girl in the green shirtdress stand up on the seat of the pew. People on both sides of the aisle were turning now, faces raised, trying to see the children past the line of white shirts.

Lynn's gaze held on Juvenal—a tall altar boy, a gentle person being used, not knowing what to do, cornered, being made to perform in the name of God's mercy.

This was *not* the way he did it.

The authority—how did she know?

She did though, somehow.

And yet she thought, But if he can do it, why wouldn't he? Right now. All these children—

She was fascinated by the spectacle of it, the prospect of what could happen. Still, she felt sorry for him and wanted to hold onto him and help him.

''Suffer the little children,'' August said, and she thought, Oh, God, wondering then if he could be sincere . . . the straggle of children well into the aisle now, inching along, dragging, bumping, pushing aluminum aids, August saying, ''Come on, that's it, come right up here'' . . . Juvenal staring at the children . . .

Juvenal with his hands folded in front of him, his hands moving apart, then touching the white surplice that hung past his hips, lowering his eyes briefly, glancing at his hands, folding them together again and raising his eyes to the children.

She had to be closer.

Bill Hill said, ''Hey—''

Lynn was gone before he could ask where she was going—across the back of the church—then caught a glimpse of her moving up the side aisle on the left.

The girl standing on the seat of the last pew, Kathy Worthington, ignored the people who had noticed her and were staring. She watched the scene developing: the children approaching the altar where August Murray waited, arms folded now, hands in the sleeves of his surplice, striking a very churchy pose. Official dignitary. The guy next to him stared at the children and didn't move, not a muscle. His hands were somewhere beneath his surplice: probably another churchy pose, though she wasn't sure. Juvenal—she would remember the name.

She would also recall, later, the first time she saw Lynn Faulkner: glancing over to see the girl in the blue-green print dress hurrying up the aisle.

Richie Baker was pushing Kenny Melkowski's wheelchair, trying not to bump the blind girl who was hanging onto the side or run into the kid ahead of them, Scotty, dragging along in his braces and arm crutches.

Richie had planned to stay in the back of the church with his baseball cap on, wait for the picnic to start—until he noticed the tall guy on the altar who looked like Al Kaline. He wondered if it was.

He had not been to mass in over two years, since starting his chemotherapy. He wasn't going to go anyplace where he had to take off his baseball cap and show his Kojak skull, which is what the kids called him and wasn't funny anymore. They called him Kojak and sometimes Lollypop and once in a while Yul Brynner. One time he cried—only once, he got so mad—and said, "You try cobalt sixty sometime and see how you like it!" But they didn't know what he was talking about. The little shitbirds. That's what his mom called them.

She'd said, "Oh, Richie," in that voice like she was in pain, "why don't you go to the picnic with the kids; it'll do you good." She was always reminding him he was sick. They'd say, "You don't look sick except your head," and laugh and ask him over and over what he had. He'd say, "How many times I have to tell you? Acute lymphocytic leukemia." And they'd say, "Big deal."

The guy *could* be Al Kaline, except what would Al Kaline be doing here? He wasn't even sure if Al Kaline was a Catholic. He hoped he was. Out of his 1,132 baseball cards, 27 of them were Al Kaline, though none of them said what religion he was and now you couldn't get them anymore; Al Kaline was announcing Tiger Baseball with George Kell and Joe Pellegrino. They were really good.

The blind girl had her face raised. She bumped into the side of Kenny Melkowski's wheelchair and Richie said, "Lookit where you're going, will you?"

He could feel everybody staring at his head. It was like he didn't have any clothes on. Just below his gaze, Kenny had so much hair—blond hair curling under, like a girl's.

The guy in the altar boy clothes was not as big as Al Kaline. He looked different now. But he looked familiar and Richie wondered if he was somebody else, on one of the other baseball cards. He thought of Fred Lynn and then Rick Burleson, both of them Red Sox—except this guy had lighter hair. Lighter than Al Kaline's too. Burleson was hitting .286.

The one taking pictures would shoot Kenny and the blind girl and then look past him, deciding, and then snap another picture.

The kid Scotty was so slow. The blind girl looked like she was staring at the ceiling.

Richie thought of Frank Tanana of the Angels, because Tanana was from Detroit and had gone to Catholic Central. Then Soderholm, White Sox third baseman, hitting .294. But Soderholm had a mustache.

The guy on the altar was looking at him. Richie didn't get it. Was he supposed to know him? The other man-altar boy on the altar was trying to motion to the one with the camera, finally stepping down into the aisle and pulling at his surplice, getting him out of the way.

Richie was looking directly at Juvenal. He wanted to go up and say something to him. But what?

He wanted to run up there and laugh with him—God—about what?

He wanted to jump on him. . . . Really?

Yeah, that's what he felt like. For no reason he could understand but simply feeling the urge very strong, in front of all these people, too, and with his bald, shining head, it didn't matter. And that's what he did.

Richie gave the wheelchair a little push, moved around it, and was past the blind girl and Scotty before he knew it, in front of everybody, running up on the altar and seeing the guy's hands coming out from under his surplice red—red?—it didn't matter, wet red, the hands taking his shoulders and the guy going down to become no taller than he was as he felt the guy's arms go around him. He was thinking something, thinking what was he doing here? But he felt good. For no reason he felt so good he wanted to jump up in the air, not even worrying about the people watching, and then run somewhere, run as fast as he could, not to get away but to be running; but he began to calm down and felt something sticky wet on the back of his T-shirt, on his arms, God, his head, and a sound, voices, voices getting louder in a sound like oooooooohhhhh or aaaaaaaaahhh and a voice saying very loud, "Lord Jesus Christ," and another one saying, "My *God*," and a sound like breath being sucked in and feet moving on the wooden floor, Richie Baker right in the middle of it looking up at the guy's face now, way up, the guy standing again, so Richie moved back and that's when he saw the hands held out from Juvenal's sides palms up, the hands full of blood.

August was saying, "Get him! *Get* him!" pulling Greg around, grabbing the Minolta from him and hurrying glancing at it to get his finger on the button and then pressing the camera to his face.

Lynn came across the front of the first pew, coming but holding back because she didn't know what she was going to do.

A woman had cried out. Words, *Jesus* and *God*, had come from the crowd, an eruption of hushed sound and now silence as Juvenal stood with his hands extending out to both sides, blood on his hands, blood on the white surplice, blood on the boy standing before him, posed—no, the pose of a man crucified but not purposely posing; he didn't know what to do with his hands, with himself, he didn't know what to *do*.

He stood waiting.

Nailed, if he was nailed at all, to where he stood. Unable to move. Then seemed about to say something, looking at the people.

What? Tell them what? Explain it—how?

Still the mild expression, but a flush of pain, holding something in. Trying to be composed, to explain it. Listen, I'm just—I'm no different—I'm—

No one in the church was going to move, perhaps ever. They stared.

Lynn walked up to him. She heard the *snick* of the

camera and looked at August. August hesitated, then lowered the camera.

She looked at Juvenal, saw his eyes.

Help me. I don't know how to do this. But in the same expression, wonderment. *Do you believe it? Look.*

Lynn reached out.

She would not look at anyone or think of anything. She would simply do it, take Juvenal's hand . . .

August said, "The children."

What did that mean? Lynn felt the blood in her own hand now, leading Juvenal down the aisle past the children and the Gray Army and the layers of faces, past Bill Hill and the girl standing on the seat of the last pew, past everyone and out the door.

Bill Hill said, "Jesus Christ."

Kathy Worthington said, "What's her name?" getting her note pad out of the canvas bag.

Within a few minutes August was distributing his pamphlets entitled "Stigmata."

People were beginning to file outside, looking around, wondering where Juvenal and the girl had gone.

15

Kathy Worthington told August at the church she'd look at his pictures, sure, bring them down; but she couldn't promise anything. He asked her how she was going to write it. She said, write what? What happened? August said here, and gave her three copies of the stigmata pamphlet plus his Juvenal story, "The Miracle Worker of the Amazon," and, for a little Outrage background, "Without Traditions Where Are We?" and "Why the Holy Ghost Flew Vatican II."

Kathy was glad to get away from the church and everybody standing around talking excitedly, blowing up what had happened bigger and bigger in their minds.

Later on, August drove downtown to the *Free Press* building on West Lafayette and walked into the city room at ten after four, surprised at all the empty desks. He had imagined reporters pausing, looking up as he walked by— "That's August Murray"—and a hush coming over a roomful of typewriter and telephone noise. But it was Sunday, with only an assistant city editor and four reporters among the wall-to-wall desks piled with files and binders and books, magazines—it looked like they were saving up for a paper drive. Kathy rose from where she was talking to some guy and led August back to her desk. He handed her a thick manila envelope.

"How can you work in a place like this?"

"What's the matter with it?" Kathy said. She opened the envelope, pulled out a stack of black-and-white eight-by-ten glossies and began going through them—crippled children outside the church . . . crippled children inside . . . Juvenal . . .

Too fast for August. He wanted to slow her down; raised up out of his chair to lean on the desk. "There he is. Look at the hands."

Kathy studied the close-shot of Juvenal, cropped at his hips, hands raised from his sides. "It doesn't look like blood."

"It's blood," August said. "You saw it on him, you saw it on the kid."

"I don't know—in the paper it's gonna look like a dark blob."

"Tell them it's blood, that's what blood looks like. 'Suddenly his hands began to bleed, blood pouring out as though nails had been driven through his palms. His side began to bleed, as though from a spear—' "

"I didn't see his side bleed. Did you?"

"It bled," August said. "When he gets the stigmata he bleeds from all five wounds, hands, side, and feet."

"Where is he now?" Kathy said.

August hesitated. "He's okay. Look, the reason I gave you the literature—read 'Miracle Worker of the Amazon,' it documents the first appearance of his stigmata when he was down in Brazil and gives the doctor's report, wounds bleeding from no natural cause, the same wounds suffered by Jesus Christ on the cross. Read the one, 'Stigmata.' "

"I did," Kathy said. "Who was that with him, his sister?"

"He doesn't have a sister."

"I thought there was a resemblance. Her name's Lynn something."

"Look," August said, "if it's not a natural phenomenon then it has to be supernatural. What else is there?"

"Unnatural," Kathy said.

"What do you mean, like from the devil?"

"Let's keep it simple," Kathy said. "No natural cause means they don't know. It could be psychosomatic; he believes it—" She paused.

"Yeah?" August waited.

Kathy had to think. "He concentrates so hard, like a mystical experience, hallucinating—"

"Yeah?"

"—that he thinks it's happening to him."

"But it *is*. We saw it," August said. "If he'd taken his clothes off, his shoes, we would have seen the five wounds of Christ crucified. He wasn't meditating or hallucinating, he was showing us that he's been singled out by God and given this special sign. You *saw* it, real blood. It wasn't ketchup, it wasn't some kind of trick."

"Most readers—"

"What?"

God, he was annoying. Sitting there, all his pens and pencils in his shirt— "Most readers won't believe it."

"You know that for a fact," August said, "or you going by some pseudo-sophisticated idea of your own? Write what you saw, that's all you have to do."

"I'll write something," Kathy said. "It's up to the city editor whether it gets in or not."

"Long as you don't slant it with all that alleged, would appear to be . . . put down what you saw. You want to quote from my stigmata pamphlet you have permission, use as much as you want."

"I'll say, according to August Murray, an unbiased source," Kathy said.

"An *honest* source, interested in the truth."

"As you see it."

"I'm talking about absolute truth, standards of

morality—'' August paused. ''What we're suffering in this
country, and I don't mean just the Church, is a . . .
pandemic erosion of ethical standards and feelings.''

''Where'd you read that?''

''Write it down, they can read it in the *Free Press*.''

''A pandemic erosion—''

''Listen,'' August said then, ''you're the one mentioned
it, using me as an unbiased source, thinking ha-ha, that's
pretty funny, like you're talking over my head. I've read
you people, everything you ever said about me you have
to put snide little jabs in. You think the people out there
buy your bullshit? They say, the good honest people, they
say, 'Who's that broad? Who does she think she is?' You
want to do a service for the people who read this
opinionated piece of shit you put out?—and I'll tell you
the only thing it's good for too—start writing the facts for
a change and quit acting like you're smarter than everybody else. That's what I advise you to do. You saw a
man with the stigmata, the marks of Christ, which haven't
appeared on a living soul in ten years, and go back to
Saint Francis of Assisi himself, the first one to ever have
it and only three hundred and twenty people since him.
Three hundred and twenty-*two* now. *You* saw it—I'll give
you that, you were the only person from the news media
who came; not even the *Michigan Catholic* was there, for
Christ sake—but that means you have a responsibility to
report exactly what you saw and tell the implications of
it.''

''What implications?''

''The fact it's a sign from God and a very probable
indication of sainthood.''

God, Kathy was thinking, any God; get me out of this.
''I'll write something,'' she said, ''and we'll see what
happens. But it's up to the editor.''

''Okay,'' August said, ''write it, keeping in mind you
have three different stories to tell.''

Kathy didn't ask what they were. She knew August was going to tell her as he held up a finger and took hold of it with his other hand.

"You got your stigmata story, miraculous marks of Christ appear the first time in this decade on a humble man, a one-time missionary by the name of Juvenal."

"That's his real name?"

"That's the name he took as a Franciscan."

"Why'd he leave the order?"

"You'll have to ask him that."

"Did they throw him out?"

"He left of his own accord."

"What's his real name?"

August hesitated. "That's up to him, if he wants to tell you."

"Do you know it?"

"Yes."

"Then why don't you tell me?"

"Because it's up to him." August was irritated now. "It's *his* name. If he wants to tell you, he will."

"Okay," Kathy said, "if I see him, I'll ask."

August settled back. He crossed his legs, resting a brown sandal with heavy straps and studs, on his knee.

"Second, you've got your Outrage story. The rapid growth of the traditionalist movement, a counterrevolution, a renaissance, rebirth of time-honored ecclesiastical and sacramental rites as they affect the more than one million Catholics in the Greater Detroit area."

Kathy scribbled something on her note pad. "I've got my stigmata and my traditionalist movement . . . what else?"

August gave the smartass reporter a tight-jawed stare, taking his time. "And you've got the miraculous healing of little Richie Baker."

"Who's Richie Baker?"

"A ten-year-old victim of acute lymphocytic leukemia,

a terminal illness he's had for two years . . . until twelve twenty-five this afternoon.''

Kathy said, ''You mean the bald-headed kid?''

''Richie Baker lost his hair from cobalt treatments, Children's Hospital. He goes there every week for therapy. Check it out.''

''Who says he's cured?''

''Talk to him; talk to his mother.''

''I mean how do you know?''

''Check it out.''

''There's no way to tell by looking at him, is there?''

''Check it out. Richie's been healed, not cured. Medical science had nothing to do with it. Go on, check it out.''

If he said it once more—Kathy laid her ballpoint on the desk. ''Okay, let me get to work.''

''There're your three stories,'' August said. ''Maybe you'll need some help.''

''We'll manage,'' Kathy said, ''somehow.'' Actually, she was thinking, there were four stories. The stigmata, the movement, Richie Baker, and a profile of a guy who carried five pens and pencils in his shirt pocket and wore socks with his Roman sandals.

She thought, How would you like to go out with him? Do the Stations of the Cross. Maybe take in a perpetual novena somewhere . . . as she began looking at the photographs of Juvenal . . . the hands . . . the face, the mild expression even as he held the blood in his hands . . . the eyes that seemed to be looking at her . . .

Kathy said, ''Hey, what're you doing?'' Not sure then if she was talking to herself or the photograph.

The good-looking black girl turned from the switchboard and came over to the desk. ''No, he doesn't answer. I know he went out this morning.''

''I picked him up,'' August said.

"Well, you know where he went then."

"And I know he came back." Because where else would he be? August held her gaze, hard-eyed, to make her tell the truth.

The good-looking black girl said, "If he did, he didn't check in and that's something he always does."

"I'll go up and look around."

"I'm afraid you won't. Less you get permission from Father Quinn."

"Call him."

"He's not here either."

"He's told me, I can go anywhere I want in this place."

"He hasn't told me."

"You know you're gonna be in serious trouble," August said, "as soon as I talk to Quinn. I hope you realize it."

"Yeah?" the good-looking black girl said, leaning on the counter now. "I never been in trouble before. Tell me about it."

August walked out and got in his black Charger standing in the no-parking zone . . . thinking of a new pamphlet he'd write.

The problem of proselytizing minorities.

He should have written it a long time ago. *Trying to reach the unreachable . . . the unteachable.*

Hell, tell it like it is.

Why there are so few niggers in the Catholic Church.

August was tired, feeling the great weight of all the work he had to do.

16

"No, it's not my real name," Juvenal said. "My real name's Charlie Lawson."

"*Charlie?* Come on," Lynn said. "Guys named Charlie don't have things like that happen to them. God, can you see it? This big statue in church—someone says, 'Who's that?' And someone else says, 'Oh, that's Saint Charlie.' "

"There was a Saint Charles," Juvenal said.

"What did he do?"

"I don't know. He probably got martyred."

"How'd you get Juvenal?"

"You pick three names when you go in," Juvenal said. "I liked Raphael or Anthony. They said, 'What else?' and showed me a list of names. I said, 'I guess Juvenal,' and that's the one they gave me, Brother Juvenal."

"Why didn't you become a priest?"

"I think I was sort of edging in, because I wasn't that sure, I mean of a vocation. I thought if for some reason I left the order as a brother it wouldn't be as bad."

"Maybe you should never have entered."

"But how else would I find out?" He seemed to shrug. "It wasn't wasted. It's still part of my life."

"Saint Juvenal," Lynn said. She paused, looking at him sitting in the cranberry crushed velvet with Waylon's face above him. He was barefoot and wearing a "shave-coat," a little blue-striped thing like a short bathrobe the TV anchorman with the hair had left behind. Juvenal didn't ask whose it was. He showered, put it on, and handed her his pants and shirt and socks to throw in the washer. There was an odor of flowers she thought was a new Oxydol scent. She had said, "Do you think it's all right?" The idea of stigmata blood going down a wash drain, remembering the scent of flowers; it was strange. He said, "It's my blood. I don't see anything different about it." She threw in the Dacron cassock and surplice, too, the scent lingering. Then washed away the blood that stained her left hand, his blood . . . and changed from the eighty-dollar dress to tight jeans and a cotton shirt, leaving the two top buttons open, answered the phone twice while he was in the shower—Bill Hill and then Artie—and unbuttoned the third button before Juvie came out.

Juvie, when she was thinking about him; Juvenal when they were talking.

He was easy to talk to, interested, he listened, looking right at her while she told him about Bill Hill and Doug Whaley and KMA Records, Artie, the Cobras, the guy from William Morris; he grinned and was like a little kid. He seemed to *know* without having things explained to him, savvy and yet naive. God, and he was a very good-looking guy, the first good-looking guy she had ever met who didn't come on with a lot of bullshit, working up to a little sack time. This one—he had an innocence about him, no pretense; like he didn't even know he was good-looking. Thirty-three years old, eleven of them spent in the Franciscans, either in a monastery or a Brazilian mission.

Could he still be a virgin? The thought hit her cold. My God, it was possible. Even with all the singles bars and casual sex, girls carrying their toothbrushes and nighties in their handbags—he had been away from all that, sheltered, protected. And if he had known before that he was going in—gotten the religious call when he was younger—he might have avoided girls. She wondered if she could ask him. By the way, are you still a virgin? The possibility intrigued her more than his stigmata. Incredible.

Looking at him on the couch—was he the same person as the one on the altar? That seemed a long time ago.

She said, "Do you suppose by any chance you're a saint?" (Was it all right to fool around with saints? It was getting heavy.)

"I don't think so," Juvenal said.

Amazing. Not laughing or saying oh, no, horrified at the thought; simply, he didn't think so.

Lynn sat on the floor looking at him across the coffee table, past the ice-cold wet Spumante bottle, watching him reach for his glass, take a sip, and ease back again in the shorty shavecoat, bare legs, bare feet— He seemed comfortable. But he always seemed comfortable. Even on the altar when he didn't know what to do. He had waited quietly for whatever would happen next.

"This is really weird, you know it?"

"You mean sitting here?"

"Yeah, I guess," Lynn said. "I mean your being here considering, well, you're a little different than most people I know. Like a celebrity."

"Not freaky?"

"No, actually, if you saw some of my friends, they're the freaks. That's what's weird, you and I sitting here— I mean after what happened, and all those people and what they must be thinking—we sit here and it seems so natural. I think to myself, How am I supposed to act with you? Should I act reverent, real serious, or what? But we just talk like, you know, it was nothing. I go, 'You suppose you're a saint?' And you go, 'I don't think so.'

All this blood pours out of you, you don't even get excited.''

"I'm getting used to it," Juvenal said. "The first few times, I was scared to death."

"I can't imagine you being scared."

"I was numb."

"Really? How many times has it happened?"

"Twenty. No, twenty-one now."

"In how long?"

"Next month will be two years."

"And you healed somebody each time it happened?"

"I think so, I'm not sure."

"What was the first time like?"

"Well, it was a little boy who was crippled. He came up to me in the street—"

"This was in Brazil?"

"Uh-huh, in a village near Santarem. The boy—I don't know why he came to me or why I touched him, but in that moment I knew something was going to happen and I wanted to run."

"God," Lynn said.

"I felt something wet—I thought the boy was bleeding. Then I saw my hands, the marks in my palms, and I saw my feet, I was wearing sandals. I couldn't believe it. Then a little girl came over—"

"Can I look at your hands?"

She rose to her knees and leaned over the coffee table as he offered his hands, palms up, lined, calloused, pink, with faint purple scars in the hollows, like marks from an indelible pencil.

"Wow. Do you always have those?"

"No, they go away."

"Well . . . what do you think?"

"What do I *think?* I told you about the stigmata, what I know."

"I mean, do you really think that's what it is?"

"What else? All five wounds—"

"Do you, like pray and think about being holy all the time?"

"I pray, yeah, but not the way I used to, or for anything in particular. It's more like talking to God."

"Do you think He hears you?"

"Sure, or I wouldn't pray."

"How do you know He does?"

"I don't *know* it, I believe it."

"Do you ever pray to a crucifix?"

"Not *to*. You pray before a crucifix," Juvenal said. "Sometimes I do, but not as a regular thing."

"Well . . . do you believe God's doing this to you?"

"He could be. Or it could be psycho-physiological, I don't know. Like when we're sad, we cry. We get mad or upset, there's a physical reaction. If my mind's causing it, then it's psychosomatic. If God's doing it, it's super-natural."

"Which do you think it is?"

"I have no way of knowing. But when you get right down to it, what difference does it make? It seems to do some good."

"You're awfully cool about it."

"I accept it, that's all. Do I have a choice? I'm not gonna pretend it's something mystical and then find out I'm psycho and should be put away."

"You don't believe that."

"No, not really. Even trying to keep an open mind."

"What did the other Franciscans say about it?"

"Down there? Nothing really. There wasn't any need to make a formal statement; most of the people believe in magic and witchcraft anyway. Some of the friars were turned on by it—Christ, a real stigmatic; let's see. The others, I guess the general reaction was stigmata, huh? No shit. And went about their business. You have to know Franciscans."

"What does that mean?"

"Well, I think for the most part they're childlike, in a good way."

"What about your superiors?"

"They said to keep quiet. They didn't want another Lourdes or Fatima on their hands, the carnival atmosphere, all the religious hucksters moving in."

"That's what Bill Hill said. Pretty soon they're setting up stands to sell Juvie dolls, or something like that."

"I'm gonna have to meet him," Juvenal said.

"He already called while you were in the shower. He wanted to come over but I told him to wait. I said I didn't know what happens next in something like this."

"Nothing happens; it's over."

"Until the next time," Lynn said. "Do you feel it coming?"

"No. Sometimes I think it's gonna happen and it doesn't."

"Have you ever healed anybody and you didn't bleed?"

"No. That's why I'm not sure which comes first. Or if they both happen at the same time."

"Does your Church know about it?"

"My Church? You mean Rome? I doubt it," Juvenal said. "But when I came home from Brazil I was sent to Duns Scotus, over on Nine Mile, west of here."

"I've seen it," Lynn said. "Gorgeous place, like a monastery."

"Yeah, it's a seminary really. I got there, I thought, fine. But then I was told not to have any communication with the students. They put me to work as a gardener. I said, Why don't you send me someplace where I can do some good? I wanted to work in a hospital." Juvenal grinned, the way Lynn's eyes opened wider. "No, not to heal anybody, I like working in hospitals, I always have. They said wait. I waited, asked a few more times, waited seven months, and walked out. Which was not the way to do it, but I did.''

"Then what? You went to the alcohol center?"

"Yeah . . . but not right away."

She expected him to continue, describe what happened next, before going to work at Sacred Heart, but he didn't. Juvenal sipped his wine and sat back; he seemed tired.

Lynn said, "You must wonder a lot, why you? Huh?"

"Once in a while. I used to all the time."

Now, she thought. And said, "You mind if I ask you a question?"

"No, go ahead."

But as he looked at her, waiting, she chickened out. "I've been asking too many questions as it is. It can wait."

"I don't mind," Juvenal said, "but I've got to be getting back pretty soon." He smiled at her. "You coming to finish your cure?"

"I've dried out," Lynn said, "but I'll take you."

They drove down Woodward instead of taking the freeway—Juvenal's idea—from the suburbs down through the wide, main inner-city street that was going to seed. Not something you'd show the out-of-town visitor. But look, there's life, Juvenal said. People. What would you rather look at, people or cement? He said he liked big cities and all the crap and confusion. He'd spot things out the car window—a black hooker propositioning a white guy in front of the Cathedral of the Most Blessed Sacrament—and smile and make mild comments.

She liked his smile, because she knew it was real. He wasn't pretending to be happy or smiling to show his teeth. His teeth were all right, but not great. When he smiled he seemed to know something. But it wasn't an I-know-something-you-*don't* smile. Like a shit-eating grin. Or like the wavy-haired Baptist preachers on TV who

smiled talking about Jesus and made you nervous. That
was a Bobby Forshay grin—gee, just so goddamn happy
because he'd been saved and knew something you didn't.
Juvenal's smile was good because he wasn't aware of it.
He seemed not to be aware of himself at all.

After five hours at Lynn's place, talking about all kinds
of things, they seemed to be talked out on the ride
downtown.

Until Juvenal said, "You were gonna ask me
something. I'll bet it had to do with . . . did I ever go
out with girls, or do I like girls or am I sort of strange
or celibate for religious reasons . . . something like that?"

"God," Lynn said, "is that part of it? You know what
people are thinking?"

"Yeah, ESP," Juvenal said. "You know how you do
it? You listen to the other person instead of thinking of
what you're gonna say next. That's all, and you learn
things."

"Like the other night in your office," Lynn said.

"Like the other night," Juvenal said. "We'd talked
earlier—I don't know, I just had a feeling you were gonna
say you were worried about breast cancer. I mean to test
me."

"Why, because you think I'm sex-oriented?"

"Because you're sort of earthy. I said, 'Your breasts
are okay,' and I'll bet you were gonna make a remark;
only you didn't."

"I was gonna say something like, 'Just okay?' and give
you a look. I mean kidding."

"Why didn't you?"

"I didn't want to sound like a smartass."

"It wouldn't have been smartass; it would've been
funny."

"Why'd you touch me?"

"Why not? We were talking about your breasts."

There was a silence. Lynn drove, looking straight ahead.

"Well, okay, I'll ask you. Do you have a hangup about girls, or what?"

"No, I like girls," Juvenal said. "But the idea of being attracted to a girl, you know, is something new. You were married, what, nine years?"

"Eight and a half."

"Well, you know something I don't," Juvenal said. "I bleed from five wounds and heal people, but I've never been in love. Isn't that something?"

17

The Monday, August 15 edition of the *Detroit Free Press* carried the story on page 3, which was like a front page of local news. There was no picture.

Miracle Claimed in Almont Church
By Kathy Worthington
Free Press staff writer

Almont, Mich.—Blood appeared on the hands of a former Franciscan missionary, known only as Juvenal, as he stood on the altar Sunday. He was about to give a special blessing to a number of crippled children in the congregation.

The bleeding was spontaneous, without an apparent cause, and was immediately acclaimed a miracle, a form of stigmata.

The scene was the dedication of St. John Bosco church as a place of worship for tradition-minded Catholics who favor the mass in Latin. They oppose, in general, Vatican-approved changes in Catholic forms of worship. About 200 were in attendance and witnessed the spontaneous hemorrhaging in the palms of Juvenal's hands.

Juvenal, about 30, had been a Franciscan brother 11

years. He served at a mission in Brazil before leaving the order last year.

Many in the church believed the phenomenon to be a true stigmata, which is described as the appearance of the wounds of Christ's crucifixion on the body of a living person. Fr. Nestor, the pastor of St. John Bosco, said, ''There is no doubt in my mind, it is stigmata.''

A pamphlet entitled ''Stigmata'' was distributed following the occurrence. Juvenal, however, was not available for questions or comments.

Theories explaining the stigmata are conflicting. Some assume it to be a miracle, a sign from God attesting to the saintliness of the one who bears the stigmata. Others claim it to be psychogenic, an emotional state of mind that causes a physiological reaction.

The last publicized stigmatic was Padre Pio, a Capuchin monk in Italy who gained world recognition as a faith healer and confessor. He died in 1968.

There was no mention of August Murray, Outrage, the Gray Army of the Holy Ghost, or the miraculous healing of little Richie Baker.

Bill Hill called Lynn first thing Monday morning and said, Okay, tell me what happened. Lynn said, Nothing, really, in a tired voice. He told her he was coming right over. Lynn said she was going to wash her hair, clean the apartment, and then go out shopping. He said have dinner with him then. Lynn said okay, if she felt up to it.

''Look. I'm the one brought you into this. Right? I want to know what you two did, spend the whole day at your place.''

''What do you mean, like did I seduce him or something?''

"What'd you talk about?"

"We talked about all kinds of things—I don't know. He's a very normal person."

"Yes, that's very normal, a person's hands start to drip blood."

"Not just his hands. I washed his clothes."

"Jesus Christ," Bill Hill said, "you washed his clothes—you didn't save 'em?"

"What was he supposed to wear, something of mine?"

"We're gonna have a talk," Bill Hill said. "I don't think you understand what you're into."

"I'm not *into* anything," Lynn said, "and if you think I'm gonna help you put him into some kind of religious freak show you're full of shit, buddy."

"I'll pick you up at noon. We'll go out and have lunch."

Lynn said, "Hey, Bill? Stuff your lunch. I don't work for you and I don't have to take your tone of voice either." She hung up.

What tone of voice? For Christ sake, what had he said to her? Nothing.

He got August Murray's address from the stigmata pamphlet, "The Holy Ghost Press," which turned out to be Zippy Printing, across from the Detroit City Airport.

August looked up from his desk and said, Yeah? Like, What do you want? He seemed to be a very sour young man.

Bill Hill told him he had been at the church Sunday and witnessed the miracle of the stigmata—not there as a parishioner but because he was a friend of Virginia Worrel's. August had never heard of Virginia, and Bill Hill sat down and told him how he had witnessed her sight restored . . . and how Virginia would be happy to give public testimony to Juvenal's healing power, if August would like to have her out to the church sometime, even though Virginia wasn't Catholic. Bill Hill said he wasn't either, but after that service Sunday he was thinking of converting.

August was a little friendlier, though still sour. He said, "The paper never used one of the pictures I gave them or even said a word about Richie Baker, after all that kid has gone through."

Bill Hill didn't know any Richie Baker. He said, "Well, what surprised me most, your name wasn't mentioned, after bringing it all about, so to speak."

August said, "Well, that didn't surprise me. Either paper—hell, any paper, they only write about me if it can be done in a putdown derogatory way, slanted."

Bill Hill said, "You have prints of the pictures you took?"

All kinds of them, eight-by-ten glossies. August showed him, good shots of Richie Baker and the kids as well as Juvie. And press releases. August had written and printed stories of exactly what happened Sunday at 12:25 P.M. in the Church of Saint John Bosco, Almont. He had sent a "press kit" this morning to both Detroit dailies, all the suburban weeklies, and the *Michigan Catholic*, daring them to print it.

Bill Hill said, "Maybe if I took a kit . . . and some of these other pamphlets you've got—"

"What for?" August said.

"I was thinking of TV," Bill Hill said. "I've got a pretty good in at WQRD. You think these pictures would show up on TV? Say next Saturday night on a nationally televised program that goes out to millions of people across the U.S.?"

Monday morning Richie Baker woke up with hair, a fine downy fuzz covering his entire skull.

His mother, Antoinette Baker, said, "Oh, my God!"

"See?" Richie said. "I told you. You didn't believe me, did you?"

His mother called Children's Hospital and talked to Richie's doctor for fifteen minutes, finally raising her voice saying, "Remission your ass. I can tell by looking at him, I'm his mother!" And, "I'm *not* raising false hopes. There's nothing false about them." She hung up hard and went out to the kitchen to get the morning *Free Press* and find the name of the person who had written "Miracle Claimed in Almont Church."

Claimed. They hadn't even said anything about the real miracle.

Antoinette Baker looked up the *Free Press* number, dialed it, and asked for Kathy Worthington. Waiting, as the phone rang, an idea came to her, and when Kathy answered Antoinette said, "I don't want you. Let me talk to the editor, or whoever your boss is."

It happened that Jack Sheehan, an assistant city editor at the *Free Press,* was looking through August Murray's press kit when he got the call from Antoinette Baker. He said, "Yeah, I'm looking at a picture of Richie right now as a matter of fact."

Sheehan liked the photos and the press releases. He liked religious revolts, conflicts in the church, and he liked alleged miracles. To get them all in one story, and a call from Richie Baker's mom at the same time, seemed a small miracle in itself, worth about three days of follow-up stories: human-interest personal reactions, interviews with the kid and his mom; their doctor's opinion; an interview with the healer, Juvenal—Christ, *Juvenal?* It kept getting better—medical opinions of the stigmata, preferably some smartass Jewish psychiatrist; a theologian's opinion of both the healing and the stigmata; brief history of people who are said to have had it; and what does August Murray, that asshole, have to do with all

this? It might even be worth four or five days plus a
feature on Sunday.

Sheehan said to Kathy Worthington, "You were
actually *there* and saw it and you give me this one-column
piece?"

"You cut it," Kathy said. "There was a little more."

"I see there's a lot more," Sheehan said. "The kid's
mother says he was healed."

"The bald-headed kid?"

"The bald-headed kid isn't bald-headed anymore,"
Sheehan said. "You started this, you get your choice.
You want the kid or Juvenal?"

"I'll take Juvenal," Kathy said, "and the theologian."

Bill Hill took his press kit and photos out west Twelve
Mile Road to WQRD-TV, Channel 3, in Southfield
(which was one of 137 affiliates of USBS, the young,
upstart United States Broadcasting System), and waited
an hour and a half to see Howard Hart.

When he finally got in Bill Hill said, "I can understand how busy you are. Your program's a honey and I
sure appreciate your taking the time. Man, a lot's
happened since I first called and called and you couldn't
see me."

"What've you got?" Howard Hart said.

Bill Hill wanted to tell the man, first, he ought to shove
his hairpiece back farther on his head instead of wearing
it like an overseas cap. Jesus, all the money the man
made and his rug looked like it came from Kmart. Bill
Hill had watched "Hartline"—or, subtitled, "Getting to
the Heart of It with Hart"—many a Saturday evening
from ten to twelve on Channel 3 and he knew the man
had absolutely no sense of humor, though he grinned once
in a while to show his caps. But, my God, the man had
a loyal following, was seen coast to coast, and got letters
from all parts of the country telling him what a loyal

American and wonderful person he was, which he often
read on the air. Howard Hart asked his guests embarrassing questions and his viewers ate it up. He got trans-
sexuals to talk about their love life, then told them they
were sick. He asked female authors if they actually did
all the filthy things they described in their novels. He
insulted, cajoled, misquoted, called General Motors
"Degenerate Motors" and Ford the "Bored Motor
Company," claiming neither gave a damn about the
common good of the "little people." He had a masked
man on who told how he broke into Greta Garbo's apartment and stole all her underwear, not touching her furs
or jewels. A Chicano girl claimed she had gotten it on
with Ozzie Nelson "a pretty lot of times" in Bakersfield—until Howard Hart accused her of being a lying
wetback, bore in and got her to deny it finally, in tears.
That kind of stuff. Some guests had walked out of
Howard Hart interviews right in the middle of the
program, one of them being Frank Sinatra, Jr. Bill Hill
heard about it but had not seen it happen.

He showed Howard Hart the photos, making brief but
hard-pointed comments.

"He raised his hands like the crucified Christ"—Bill
Hill extended his—"and the blood poured out on the
altar."

"And on the kid, it looks like," Howard Hart said,
bent over his big kidney-shaped desk studying the photos.

"On that poor little boy," Bill Hill said, and paused.
"Who was going to die of cancer until Juvenal touched
him."

"Who says?"

"They believe it. I talked to his mom," Bill Hill said,
"a lovely woman name of Antoinette . . . divorced,
working hard to raise her boy and get him his treatments—"

"What's she do?" Howard Hart asked.

Bill Hill had him and knew it. He sat back, looking across the expensive desk at the man's $49.95 hairpiece and said, "Would you believe it? His mom's a topless go-go dancer."

Howard Hart reached over, flicked a button on his intercom and told his girl to hold the calls.

Work, work, work. But damn, he felt good. Bill Hill was promoting people again and not some dead-ass technical specs, which camper body to put on your GMC pickup bed.

Down at the Sacred Heart Center he handed Father Quinn a certified check for two hundred dollars, saying just a little something in the fight against alcoholism.

Quinn said, "You can't buy your way in here."

"I just want to see him a minute," Bill Hill said.

"The line forms up in the coffee shop," Quinn said.

The priest took him up and showed him, pausing to glance in through the doorway. There was August Murray. There, a girl from the *Free Press*. Bill Hill said yes, he knew her from church. The guy with her, a photographer. The others were from the *News*, the *Michigan Catholic*, the *Oakland County Press*, and International News Service.

"My purpose," Bill Hill said, "unlike theirs, is not to beat on him with embarrassing personal questions. I've had my own faith ridiculed in the press and I know why he's skittish."

"I know when I'm getting conned, too," Quinn said, "but at least you don't act bored and cynical. I'll see what he says."

Once your luck gets a little momentum, Bill Hill believed, there was no telling where it could take you.

Like outside to the Center's rooftop sundeck and a panoramic sweep of downtown, from Stroh's Brewery to the tall glass tubes of the Renaissance Center rising 700 feet in the air.

He said to Juvenal, who was sitting in a striped canvas chair with his shirt off, "I know what you're going through."

Juvenal said, "I doubt it. I'm not going through what you're thinking."

His body was white, his arms tan. Bill Hill didn't see a mark on his side, or on his bare feet, either.

"Maybe I can still help you," Bill Hill said.

Juvenal looked up at him. "You know why I said I'd talk to you?"

"Because you're considerate."

"Because you're a friend of Lynn's."

"She's a sweetheart, isn't she," Bill Hill said.

"I wondered how close you two are."

"Like—" Bill Hill started to hold up two crossed fingers. He let his hand drop. Jesus—the guy staring at him, serious, waiting to hear what he'd say.

"I'm like an old uncle," Bill Hill said, "interested in what she does, protective—Why?"

"I just wondered," Juvenal said.

"She's certainly taken with you," Bill Hill said. He was thinking on his feet now, feeling his way along. "She told me how . . . natural you two are together. She said, though, 'How come he hides instead of coming out and revealing himself. If God has given him this special gift, why would he keep it a secret?' "

Bill Hill was also taking a chance. What if Juvenal had already given her an answer? But he didn't have time to fool around. He had to get to the point, and quick, with all those newspaper people set to jump on the poor guy.

"I tried to explain it to her," Bill Hill said. "I told her you work here because it's an ideal place to remain anonymous; the word is understood and respected here . . . if that's what you want. If you don't, if you want to reveal yourself, so to speak, well, you could let August Murray represent you and issue statements and whatnot, act as your press agent.''

"Why would I want a press agent?''

"I wouldn't think you would. But I have a feeling that's the way somebody like August would handle it, as a promotion, and catch a ride himself for whatever he can get out of it.''

"Why can't I stay the way I am?'' Juvenal said.

"Because the news people won't let you. They've caught a glimpse of you and they won't let go till they've seen the whole thing, and picked you apart.'' He tried something else then. "I *would* think you'd like to step out into the world more, maybe see all you've been missing the past eleven years . . . get a taste of life, so to speak. I could be wrong.''

"I'm curious about some things,'' Juvenal said.

"But if you're gonna be out there you'll want a true image of yourself preceding you, not sly rumors and accusations that you're some kind of freak.''

Juvenal said, "Quinn suggested he and I go down and talk to them, make some kind of statement.''

"That's fine, you're gonna have to do something like that just to be nice,'' Bill Hill said. "But then after they run their stories, that's when you get reactions. See, people will have a feeling it isn't the *whole* story—is this guy a fake or what?—or necessarily both sides of the story if it's controversial; because your great majority of people haven't heard it from you, what you feel and think.''

"And you have a way to solve that,'' Juvenal said, sounding a little tired.

"Maybe,'' Bill Hill said. "See, you read a newspaper account, you say, 'Hey, I didn't say that. They turned it around.' Or they quote you out of context and you sound dumb. What I was thinking, what if you were in a position to tell your story personally to everybody, and I mean millions of people, and take as long as two hours if you want.''

''What's my story?'' Juvenal said.

''Touching people,'' Bill Hill said. ''You touch people and they change. I don't mean just the sick and infirm.'' Bill Hill paused. ''Didn't you know that? Take Lynn for instance—''

18

Tuesday, feature stories appeared in both the *Detroit News* and the *Free Press*. Lynn got out her scissors.

"Miracle at Almont?"

The basic story of what had taken place Sunday now emphasized the fact August Murray had distributed a pamphlet entitled "Stigmata" following the supposedly "unscheduled incident on the altar." The story cited August Murray's record of arrests as a right-wing religious activist, but did not delve into the purpose of traditionalist movement.

"Former Missionary Describes Mysterious Bleeding."

With a three-column cut of Juvenal, hands raised, eyes staring out from the photo. The news story was from the Sacred Heart Center press conference and interview. It presented the facts accurately, Lynn felt, though some of the quotes didn't sound as though they came from Juvenal. Words in there like *viable* and *preternatural*.

"Stigmata: The Church's View."

An interview with Father Dennis Dillon, SJ, Associate Professor of Theology at the University of Detroit. "There exists no intrinsic relationship between sanctity and stigmatization, though God can confer charisma on anyone He chooses, even one outside the Church or in the state of mortal sin . . . according to Pope Benedict XIV.''

Lynn thought that was big of him.

". . . but is generally attributed to purely natural causes, as long as the contrary has not been proved.'' The Church, therefore is "cautious in attributing stigmatization to a miracle . . . for psycho-physiological sciences may, in the future, show such attribution to be untenable.''

So that, Lynn decided, the guy really didn't say anything.

"Stigmata: A Psychiatrist's Appraisal."

An interview with Dr. Alan Kaplan, M.D., Ph.D., author of *Psychoanalysis: Trick or Treatment.* According to Kaplan stigmatization was the result of a highly emotional, hyper-ecstatic state. "Hey, the Catholics don't have a corner on stigmata,'' said Kaplan. "The wounds Mohammed received, battling for the spread of his faith, have appeared on Moslem ascetics. And how about, a few years ago, the little ten-year-old girl in Oakland, California? She woke up Good Friday morning with the stigmata, after reading about the crucifixion and seeing a TV movie on it. The little girl's a Baptist, and she's black.'' Kaplan cited other examples of spontaneous hemorrhaging, each case involving a person "of strong hysterical disposition.'' It was like saying, What else is new?

But Juvenal didn't have a hysterical disposition. Did he?

" 'I Was Too Healed,' says Richie."

In the three-column photo Richie was touching the fuzz that covered his head, eyes raised, while his mother smiled proudly. "As soon as we saw Richie's hair we knew it was a miracle,'' said Mrs. Antoinette Baker of Clawson. "We got right down on our knees to thank the good Lord for what He had done for us.'' The news story told that Richie had returned to Children's Hospital, where a complete physical failed to reveal any trace of leukemia cells lurking in his blood or bone marrow. Said an attending physician in hematology, "We would not state categorically the impossibility of a remission not lasting indefinitely—"

Lynn read that part over three times.

"—but we strongly advise the continuance of chemotherapy at this point in time. A relapse is usually fatal." That was plain enough. But Mrs. Baker insisted, no more treatments, convinced there was no need "for Richie and I to keep going down there every Thursday when he's been healed." She added yes, she would like to meet this Juvenal sometime and thank him personally for the precious gift of life he has given them.

Then a final word from the doctor stating that no, observing the amount of hair that grew in on Richie's head overnight could not be considered usual.

In the "Accent on Living" section of the *News* was a story Lynn read through twice—beneath a four-column shot of Antoinette Baker in a bikini striking some kind of a jivey pose.

"Go-go Dancing Pays . . . Barely."

How does the divorced mother of an eleven-year-old leukemia victim, with talent but no formal training in a profession, get by these days? "Barely," says Toni Baker, "but we make it and, gosh, now, it seems too good to be true. With Richie healed I'll be able to sleep in Thursdays, my day off, and get some much-needed rest." Toni dances at the popular Caprice Lounge on Grand River, "interpreting" today's disco beat as she feels it, to the hearty approval of the gentlemen in the audience. . . . But how does a go-go dancer feel about miracles and divine intervention? Can she handle it all right? "Easy as pie," says Toni. "God gave me my

body, I'm not ashamed of it. As for miracles, well,
who knows what God's plan is for us here on, you
know, earth. I believe like if a certain person has the
power, like in *Star Wars,* you know, the 'Force,' then
they can do all these neat things to help humanity."
Toni said she and Richie were supposed to meet
Juvenal soon . . .

Which was different than the other story, Lynn noticed,
where the mother had said she'd *like* to meet him.

. . . and she was looking forward to it. She thought he
had nice eyes and was real cute, "especially for a
person who performed miracles."

When Lynn read it the second time she made comments
to herself. After ". . . no formal training in a profession
. . ." she said, You didn't need training peddling your
ass. "God gave me my body, I'm not ashamed of it."
Lynn's thought was, And this mother's giving it to everybody else.

She was irritated, she thoroughly disliked the woman,
and had to stop and analyze the feeling. Was it resentment? The book—one of the how-to-be-happy books—said
if you were disturbed or felt resentment, it was your own
fault. You didn't have to feel that way. No—

But how come all of a sudden this Antoinette Baker—
Toni now, with everybody getting to know her and love
her—was becoming the star of the show? She didn't have
a thing to do with what was going on. Nothing. But there
she was hanging out of her string bikini—way too old to
be wearing something like that, she had to be thirty-two
at least—on the front page of the *Detroit News* "Accent
on Living" section.

It burned Lynn up.

* * *

It made August Murray sick to his stomach. He said, "Look at her."

Greg Czarnicki said, "She's a little old, but not too bad."

"Look at all this," August said. He swept the newspapers from his father's desk, sweeping with them the start of a pamphlet he was writing entitled "You Claim to Be a Catholic . . . Prove It!" and a twelve-inch plaster statue of the Infant of Prague.

August and Greg looked down at the broken figure, the crowned head rolling away from the robed body of baby Jesus.

"Look what she made me do!"

"Who?" Greg said.

"That *cunt*"—Richie's mom in the bikini—"and the other one, at the *Free Press*. I gave her *every*thing, the entire story. Do you see one word about Outrage or Pius X?"

"I thought this Juvenal might mention it," Greg said, "if he's supposed to be so tuned in, or whatever you want to call it, and sympathetic."

"It's not his fault," August said, "you can't even get near him. That alcoholic priest, he actually pushed me away. I said, 'I have to talk to him.' He said, 'Come back some other time, he's got work to do.' I said, 'Yes, he's got work to do, for the *Church*, not for a bunch of drunks.' "

"What did he say?"

"I don't know—he walked out, took Juvie with him. Tomorrow you'll be reading all about Sacred Heart Rehabilitation Center and the great job they're doing—that guy Quinn, you can see it, he's gonna *use* Juvie, get all the publicity he can for his drunk tank."

Greg Czarnicki was picking up the newspapers, piling the sections neatly on the corner of the desk. "You want to save these?"

August wanted to but said no.

Greg was studying a section of the paper, holding it as he read something on the page. "There was a robbery at City Airport—you see it? They caught the guys."

"There robberies all around here," August said. "Look at them, they get their pictures in the paper with their big hats on, punk nigger kids grinning at you. You know why they're grinning? They know they'll be back on the street in a few days, looking around . . . what's a good place to break in next? You know what I hope? I hope they try to get in here sometime."

August pulled open the middle desk drawer, took out a revolver, and laid it on his writing paper, his notes and starts of pamphlets.

Greg looked at it.

"It's my dad's," August said. "Thirty-eight Smith and Wesson Commando. You think this wouldn't stop them?"

"Just scare them," Greg said. "You wouldn't actually shoot anybody, would you?"

"If he was coming in here to take something that belongs to me?" August said. "I'd shoot to kill. And if God wants to have mercy on his soul that's up to Him. You bet I'd shoot."

On Tuesday, Bill Hill went back to WQRD-TV and had to wait forty minutes this time to see the mighty Howard Hart, Bill Hill thinking, as he sat there, Go ahead, chickenfat, keep me waiting.

Boy, he hated to wait for people, especially a man who had a bloated opinion of himself, no sense of humor, and a fourth-place rating among Saturday night shows.

Howard Hart had newspapers open on his desk. Even the *Michigan Catholic*. He said, "Now what?"

"This Juvenal is a simple, honest man," Bill Hill said, "maybe even a little naive, not used to the bright lights."

"I think I'll have Richie and his mother on first,"

Howard Hart said, "then bring the doctor on. Maybe give a full hour to them. But that's something I'll feel as I go along. Then bring Juvenal on with the psychiatrist and let 'em tangle asses."

"He's a gentle person," Bill Hill said. "I think he deserves your full attention."

"The theologian, I don't know," Howard Hart said. "What side's he on, the guy's?"

"He's not on either side."

"Then I don't need him. I want to see the guy and the psychiatrist *mano a mano.*"

"Why don't you leave the psychiatrist out of it," Bill Hill said, "just talk to Juvenal."

"Why don't we leave you out instead," Howard Hart said.

"No, I got it," Bill Hill said. "Why don't you talk to the kid and his go-go mom, the doctor, the psychiatrist, *and* the theologian all this Saturday. Set it up, set the stage. Then next Saturday have Juvie on for the entire two hours."

"What do I talk to him about for two hours?"

"Anything you want. But with about fifteen minutes to go, you know what happens?"

"Tell me."

"In front of you and fifty million people, if your network's any good and can do its promotional work . . . Juvie will get the stigmata, bleed from his five wounds, and heal a cripple of your choice . . . *live* on national television."

Howard Hart had to think about that a minute; he had to try to picture it.

As he did, Bill Hill said, "Queen for a night. The chance to see your ratings shoot up from fourth place to first. It wouldn't hurt you, would it?"

"What do you know about ratings?"

"Nothing. But I read in the TV column in the paper

you're about to get canceled if your audience doesn't pick up.''

"What if the guy doesn't produce?" Howard Hart said.

"What if you had Neil Diamond on and all of a sudden he couldn't sing a note?" Bill Hill said. "This is what Juvie does, he performs miracles. If you'd rather watch him on another network, let me know right now." Bill Hill started to get up.

"Let's say I agree," Howard Hart said, thoughtful, as though he were still undecided.

"Then you hand me one of your standard contracts," Bill Hill said, "stating you'll pay me one million and forty thousand dollars for the delivery of Juvenal the miracle worker."

Howard Hart threw his head back and laughed and laughed, then shook his head and pretended to wipe tears from his eyes.

Bill Hill waited until he was through.

He said, "You got a whole bunch of commercials on your two-hour show. I counted thirty-one times including the station breaks, and I understand the network sells its time for about a hundred and twenty-five thousand dollars a minute. That's a lot of money. I want a million forty thousand of it."

"You don't know what you're talking about," Howard Hart said. "It isn't that simple."

"Then it's up to you to make it simple," Bill Hill said, "so I can understand it. We won't get into residuals on reruns, I'll talk to my lawyer and let you know what kind of a cut we want. But as it stands now, I sign for a million forty thousand or you don't get your miracle worker. Somebody else does. Or, if you try to tamper with Juvie or reach him except through me, the deal is automatically off and you're out. You want him or not?"

"What's the forty thousand for?" Howard Hart said.

"Waiting in the lobby while you read the paper. A thousand dollars a minute."

"Well—" Howard Hart sighed. "It's gonna take a few days."

"That's all I'm giving you," Bill Hill said. "Signed by Friday or no deal."

He walked out, certain of getting his contract. The secret, he'd tell Lynn, was knowing how to talk to big shots. Give them the same shit they gave everybody else.

Something else happened that Tuesday, August 16, 1977. Elvis Presley died.

19

"'**S**top it,' shrieked a grandmother in a wheat-colored pantsuit. 'I can't take any more.' The radio clicked off but her weeping didn't stop."

Bill Hill sat on the couch reading aloud from the paper.

"It says he was laid out in a simple white tuxedo with a silver tie."

Lynn was in the kitchen. She said, through the counter opening, "I read Harmony House sold out his albums, three hundred and fifty of 'em, by ten-fifteen yesterday morning."

It was 2:35 P.M. now, Thursday.

Lynn was trying to act natural: in the kitchen cutting up celery and carrot sticks, opening a bag of corn chips and putting some in a bowl . . . finishing what she had been doing when she heard the door buzz and jumped, then had gone in to buzz the downstairs door and waited, and must have looked surprised when she saw it was Bill Hill. ("No, I'm not mad at you. No, nothing's wrong. . . . Yes, as a matter of fact, I *am* expecting somebody. . . . None of your business, if you don't mind." With a snippy tone that didn't even sound like her. Then, trying to be nice, "You want to sit down for a minute?") Bill Hill had been sitting in there at least fifteen minutes now and it was almost twenty to three.

" 'Michele Leone, thirty-two, of East Detroit, called the White House and urged President Carter to decree a national day of mourning.' "

He wasn't dumb, Lynn was thinking. If he knew somebody was coming and she didn't want him here— But he kept reading to her.

"Here's one. ' "I got goose pimples," said Jane Freels of Livonia. "I felt numb. But I didn't cry till I played 'Love Me Tender' and heard his voice. My little girl, Shannon, stared at me like she was frightened and kept saying, 'What's wrong, mummy?' " ' "

Just tell him to leave, that's all.

" ' "I was talking to my other married girl friends today and they said nobody feels like doing anything. They're just numb. We just watch TV waiting to see if they're going to show anything about him. We just can't get over this." ' "

I can't either, Lynn thought, if he doesn't get the hell out of here. Doesn't call or anything, just walks in—

" ' "He was the king of rock and roll," Jane concluded, with tears in her blue eyes. "He started it all. He made us what we are today." ' Is that a tribute," Bill Hill said, "or is that a tribute? You imagine the money they're gonna make on his records and stuff? They're selling Elvis Presley memorial T-shirts, pennants—the guy that's making them says, 'I know he would've liked them.' "

"Too bad you're not down there." Lynn put the carrots and celery in the refrigerator, looked around the kitchen, and came out to the living room.

Bill Hill was saying, well, things were happening up here, too. "For us, anyway, you and I. But you better sit down if I'm gonna tell you about it, because you're not gonna believe it at first and when you do you're liable to faint."

"You didn't bring a hat, did you?"

"You're cute," Bill Hill said. "Call whoever it is and tell him you're busy. Jesus, I hope it isn't the guy with the hair on Channel Seven. You got more class than that."

"You mind if we don't discuss my personal affairs?" With the snippy tone again that she didn't like. It was hard to keep her voice natural.

"If you want to be that way," Bill Hill said. He watched her walk over to the sliding glass door and look out at the fairway, then turn, restless, gather up the newspapers from the coffee table, then not know what to do with them. "If you don't want to be partners again—"

"We were never partners before."

"—and together find success and happiness, not to mention a whole lot of money."

"Leave him alone," Lynn said. "That's all I've got time to say to you right now. Leave the poor guy alone and let him do what he wants."

"You just said it, 'the poor guy,' " Bill Hill said. "For him to be poor and left alone is not only dumb, it's a sin; because when you're gifted and you don't take advantage of the gift and use it, you know what that's like? It's like an insult to Almighty God, telling Him you don't want the gift. 'Keep it, Lord, I want to be left alone and hide out in some monastery or alcohol center.' "

"Bill, leave. Okay?"

He got up, studying her with a relaxed, confident expression, straightening his tan trousers and short-sleeved safari jacket.

He said, "You look nice, you know it? You ought to dress up more."

"I'm not dressed up."

"Those are good-looking slacks, nice fit—nice starched white blouse. You ought to throw those cutoffs and that

Bob Marley T-shirt away. And take Waylon down, get a nice painting.''

"Bill?''

"I'm going. Have a nice time with your boyfriend.''

Lynn's two-bedroom-with-balcony apartment was on the second floor of a four-unit tan brick building that was less than ten years old. In the mile-square complex of the Somerset Park Apartments—with its curving streets, sweeping lawns, its golf course, tennis courts, swimming pools—all the buildings were two stories, beige, tan, or gray, cleanly styled with sort of mansard roofs. The front door of each building was always locked. A visitor pushed the button opposite one of the four names and the front door was buzzed open from inside the apartment.

At ten after three, Lynn heard the sound and jumped—again, even though she was expecting it—as anxious, excited, as she had ever been in her life.

She buzzed the door and went out into the hall to wait, facing the stairway, the wrought-iron railing, the cathedral window that rose from the landing—the turn in the stairway—all the way up to the ceiling. The sun was streaming in through the window. It was quiet. It was perfect.

Juvenal came up the stairs, smiling. Not looking around, smiling right at her.

20

"How'd you get here?"

"They let me use a car."

"You found it all right?"

"Sure. I was here before."

"But I drove. You know, unless you were paying attention—"

"I remembered."

"Well, you look good."

"So do you."

"I was surprised when you called—"

"I had to get out of there. All the people coming to see me, even *Time* magazine and *Newsweek,* I couldn't believe it. It got so the news people were taking over the coffee shop." Juvenal paused, waited, looking at her. "That's not the reason I came though."

"I know," Lynn said.

"I came because I wanted to see you. In fact—do you want to know the truth?"

"Tell me."

"I was dying to see you."

She wasn't sure who moved first. Her arms went around his body and his arms gathered her in close, around her shoulders; she could feel his hands on her back. They held each other very tightly, standing in the hall, the sun coming in. They had reached this point almost immediately, after only brief moments of looking at each other, making opening remarks, barely able to wait, because they both knew and felt it and didn't have to hint or fool around or be coy about it. They both knew. They wanted to hold each other as tightly as they could and that's what they were doing. For the moment there was nothing else.

"I was dying too," Lynn said.

"I couldn't wait. I couldn't get out of there fast enough."

"Let's go inside, okay?"

He said, "Just a second."

She raised her face. His face was there, eyes looking into eyes, to see the person in there. They began kissing each other's mouths, moving their heads and sliding gently and getting the soft fit, trying to get inside and be lost in each other. Was it possible?

They held and kissed again, without moving, standing in the living room.

They held and kissed on the cranberry couch with Waylon above them and the newspaper accounts of Elvis on the coffee table . . . Lynn a young girl again kissing, necking—no, it wasn't necking, it was kissing and feeling it as though for the first time, kissing for kissing, not to lead to something else, though it was going to, she knew. There were things she wanted to say to him but didn't want to speak now unless she could whisper very, very quietly and not interrupt the mood or the silence. For a moment, a split moment, she saw herself alone again, after, and was afraid.

He said to her, very close but looking at her, both of them low on the couch, half sitting, half lying, he said that he loved her. He said, "I love you," in a way she had never heard before in her life. "I love you."

Lynn said, "I love *you*." And then tried it again, "I

love you. Either way, it's true. *Any* way you can say it. But I wasn't prepared. I mean I knew I loved you, but I wasn't prepared to say it. I don't want to talk yet.''

He said, ''Boy, it's good.''

She said, ''I want to feel you. I'm dying to. Can I feel you?''

He said, ''I want to feel *you*. I want to see you.''

She put her hand on his groin, on the tight, hard bleached denim. ''I feel you. There you are, right there. Part of you.''

He put his hand on her breast. ''I feel you.''

''You felt me before.''

''No, I wasn't feeling you then.''

''I know you weren't.''

''I'm feeling you now. You feel so good. That's you, isn't it?''

Her hand moved up to unbutton the buttons of his shirt and slid into the opening, her fingers brushing his side that had bled, moving up to his chest. ''I love your body. I saw your body and I loved it and now I love it more.''

He said, again, ''I want to see you. Where are you?''

''I'm here.''

He unbuttoned her blouse and opened it.

''You said my breasts were okay.''

They were smiling at each other.

''Your breasts are beautiful. Your breasts are the most beautiful things I've ever seen. They're not *things*, but I can't think of a good word. The most beautiful breasts I've ever seen—no, because that's not right.''

She was looking at him with a question, a doubt, hesitant.

He said, ''Don't think. Don't talk now.''

She said, ''I love you so much. But I don't want you to feel—you know, after, that I'm making you do something.''

He said, ''What I feel, I feel good. Listen, do you

want me to tell you exactly how I feel, if I can, how much I love you and how I feel when I'm with you?'' He was brushing her face with his mouth. ''Do you want to talk about what we're doing or do you want to just be here and that's all, because I think it's enough. I can say I've never said this before to anyone. I have no practice, no moves . . . let's take our clothes off . . . do you say that or do you just take them off or do you say something romantic first? . . . No, don't tell me, because what difference does it make . . . if you've never done this before you think, well, there's only one way to do it, not several ways. How many ways can you take off your clothes? You can tell me that.''

Lynn said, ''Come on with me.''

She said, ''God, I love you.'' She said, ''I love you so much, I don't believe it. Like it can't be happening.''

They were lying on her double bed with the top sheet and the spread thrown back, the window shade pulled, the bedroom dimly more light than dark.

He said, ''It's happening. I'm pretty sure it is.'' Lying on his back he moved his right hand to her thigh and brought it up slowly between her legs. ''Yes, it's still happening, I can feel it.''

''We're lucky,'' Lynn said. ''Right now we are.''

''You sound very solemn.''

''You're right, I've got to watch that,'' Lynn said. ''The most important thing you can do in life is not take it too seriously. I wrote that down once.''

''Why?''

''Because it's true.''

''Who said it?''

''It was Errol Flynn in a movie called *Escape Me Never,* with Ida Lupino.'' When Juvenal turned his head to look at her, Lynn said, ''I'm not trying to be funny. It was in the movie and I remember it. On television.''

"On television," Juvenal said. "Well . . . I think it's all right to take serious things seriously. As long as you don't wail and gnash your teeth. Or kick and scream. The problem is figuring out what's serious and what isn't."

She was looking at him now, her head turned on the pillow. "Are you trying to tell me something?"

He said, "I think what I'm saying is, being in love is serious and making love to the person you love must be the best thing there is. You lose yourself completely. It's awesome when I think about it." He smiled, moving against her. "But it's also a lot of fun it's so good. What I'm trying to say is that being serious doesn't mean you have to be solemn."

"My instant reaction," Lynn said, "I want to say, But it's too good to be true."

"Or, it's so good that it's true," he said. "Unless, for some reason, you want to be sad."

"Did you read that?"

"No, I didn't read it. I don't think I did."

"I have a terrible feeling that when something good happens it's not gonna last," Lynn said. "But when I look back, the good things that've happened to me haven't been all that good. So it doesn't matter they didn't last. But now—do you know what I mean?"

"Well, you told me you're not in love with anybody else."

"God, no."

"You don't have any binding commitments."

"None."

"I don't either," Juvenal said, "so what's the problem? I haven't read any book on this, I'm feeling my way along"—and smiled at her as his hand moved gently into the hollow of her stomach and down to the patch of soft hair between her legs—"you might say, going by instinct. But are you supposed to worry about it? Why can't we just accept what's happening and say fine?"

She said, "But you're not just someone, some guy—"

"Sure I am. I'm Charlie Lawson—and I haven't heard that in a long time. You want, you can call me Charlie."

"You're more than that, a name."

"How should I act then?"

"You were in a religious order—"

"I came out. Priests come out now, get married, it doesn't seem to bother anyone."

"You're *dif*ferent."

"Right, I wasn't even a priest."

"You know what I mean, you *bleed*. God, I'm lying here with you—from the same as Christ's wounds—do you realize, would you like to try to look at it from over here? Put yourself in my place."

"I bleed from my own wounds," Juvenal said. "They aren't even wounds. I bleed from my mind, who knows? Or God makes it happen. Maybe. But there aren't any conditions, rules of behavior. It happens to *me*, so how do I handle it? What do I do? I accept it—I told you that—because I don't have any other choice." He paused. "What else? I touch people—" He paused again. "And you touched me. You took my hand—"

"I want to be with you," Lynn said, "but I don't want to be in your way. This is something, it's way over my head and I guess that's part of what I mean I don't believe it's happening. You have to understand, I was married to a *saddle* bronc rider.

"You want me to pretend to be pious?"

"You act like it's nothing."

"If it's mine, if it's happening to me—" His voice was very quiet as he said, "How do you want me to act?"

"I don't know." She closed her eyes, to rest or run away for a moment.

He waited until she opened them again.

"I don't know either. But if there aren't any rules, why can't I be myself?"

"Maybe . . . your Church won't let you."

"You mean a person in the Church? Who?"

"Well, what if—and I'm serious—what if it turns out you're a saint?"

"What if I am? What if we both are? We'll be canonized in two hundred years and young girls will pray to Saint Lynn. Will you intercede for them, take their petitions to God?"

"Is that how it works?"

"Who knows? What do we know that we're sure of? I'll tell you the only thing I know and can feel and believe," Juvenal said, "I love you, I want to be with you."

"But why?"

"Because I've known you all my life and maybe even before that and I feel good with you. I'm beginning to know what it means to feel one with another person. I don't mean making love, and that's an unbelievable experience, making love with someone you love; but it's part of it, trying to be physically one with your bodies"—looking at her body now—saying, "I love your body," and smiling at her. "I'm talking more than I've ever talked in my life. Let's make love to each other again."

It was in Lynn's mind to say, "You're really something," or "You're too much." But she didn't. She smiled back at him and said, "Okay."

He slept. Lynn lay awake. She would look at him and slowly look away from him and catch glimpses of the other two, the ones from the TV channel and the radio station. But it wasn't the same thing, what she did with him and what she did with them. He said you lose yourself in each other and that's what it was like, being with-him in-him while he was in her, feeling him and feeling herself as one, not wanting it to end it was so good—and it didn't end because they clung together after for a long time, mouths touching, brushing, and the after was another experience in itself and could go on for a long time, as long as they wanted, until they smiled and touched places and began at the beginning again. But it wasn't like that with the other two. It was an act with the other two with a beginning and an end and awareness of where she was and what she was doing and what they were doing—"Do you like that?" "Uh-huh"—every step of the way. She had never closed her eyes and fantasized, imagined the man was someone else. She could have done it with the other two, because there was room in her mind to fool around with fantasies or think of appointments or movies. But not with the man lying beside her now, who knew nothing of pretense or that men must appear to excel at this and leave the girl exhausted as they lay back or rolled over—there, that's done. She thought, What did you expect from them?

And then thought, Don't put them down.

See? She felt different with Juvenal, being with him. His kindness rubbed off on her, his innocence . . .

But he had said something . . .

Talking about it being an unbelievable experience, making love to someone you love. And he'd said it before that, in the living room, about the seriousness of it, loving someone and making love to the person.

As opposed to making love to . . . someone you didn't love? How would he know the difference?

In the kitchen, reading the Jiffy Pop label, she was wearing bikini panties and an apron that covered her breasts in front but left them bare on the sides . . . where his hands slipped in from behind and took hold of her after pulling open the tie strings.

"I like your outfit."

She relaxed against him, dropping the Jiffy Pop on the

counter and reached around to feel his bare legs. "What do you have on; nothing?"

"My drawers."

"Nuts."

"You're close." He said then, "I'll ask you one question, okay? Is this how people talk?"

"It's how we talk."

"I feel like I can say anything I want to you and you won't laugh or think it's dumb, even if it is."

"I don't think there's a book on it," Lynn said. "I don't think people who write how-to books say goofy things. I don't know, maybe they do. When you're alone you can say anything you want, nobody's listening to us. But even if they were—"

"You're right. Who cares?"

"Can I ask you one?"

"Sure."

She hesitated, then said, "Have you met Antoinette Baker yet?"

"Yeah, she and Richard came—you know everybody calls him Richie and he doesn't like it. I had a feeling— I called him Richard when I met him and saw him light up a little bit. Then when we were talking he told me, he hates Richie, the name."

"Did you like her?"

"The mother? I didn't dislike her. But that's not what you were gonna ask me."

"You're scary, you know it?"

"Have I ever made love before to anyone. Why couldn't you ask that?"

"It's none of my business."

He turned her around to face him, his hands on her hips, fingers touching the elastic top of her pants.

"I did. Sort of."

"It's not something you do *sort of*. But, listen, you don't have to tell me."

"I do now. Who knows what you'll imagine. Right?"

"Did you like her?"

He hesitated now. "I liked her, yes. Her name was Annie, twenty years old—we spent the night in a motel."

"How did you meet her?"

"In a bar downtown. She was a prostitute."

"Oh—"

"I didn't know it at first. We were talking—I liked her because she seemed very open, she was funny, a nice-looking girl."

"You spent the whole night together?"

"Uh-huh. I was drunk. I don't mean that as an excuse—I was very curious about the girl, about going to bed with her and all, finding out what it was like—but the being drunk, during that period, right after I left the order and walked out of Duns Scotus, I was drunk most of the time for about three weeks."

"I can't imagine you drunk."

"That's why I finally went to Sacred Heart. I thought I was an alcoholic."

"But you weren't."

"I was a third-rate amateur. Do you know what alcoholics call New Year's Eve? Amateur night. I was thinking too much, going around in circles, beating on myself for leaving the order and trying to work up a good feeling of guilt, because that's what I thought I *should* feel, guilty. Quinn straightened me out in about three days. He said I could stay if I wanted, as long as I wanted and . . . here we are."

"It didn't take you long."

"I wasn't that bad off. I just had to resolve the guilt thing."

"You don't feel it now?"

He smiled. "You mean with you? No. There might've been more to it than guilt; I suspect there was, anyway.

But I have no reason to dig around in the past to find out what it is.''

"Do you think about the girl?''

"No. I barely remember what she looked like, except she had dark hair, she was small, pretty.''

"A pretty whore.''

"What's the matter with that?''

"Nothing. See, that's a prejudice coming out, a little smart-assness. The thing is, I'm really glad you told me, because then I don't feel like the only one who's fooled around, but I don't like to think of you with someone else.''

"Then don't.''

"I've never been jealous before,'' Lynn said. "It's a new feeling, having something I want more than anything—that's why I'm afraid it's gonna end, something will happen.''

"Like what?''

"I don't know, something.''

Serious, in a see-through apron and panties . . .

Then both dressed, in the living room again with beer and wine, corn chips and dip, popcorn and the celery and carrots, and they were smiling again and saying whatever they wanted, dumb or not, because it didn't matter, they were playing, having fun . . . Lynn telling him about the 117-foot World's Tallest Illuminated Cross of Jesus and the battery-operated replicas and the WTICOJ T-shirts and what a hotshot promoter Bill Hill was in his day.

They might have stayed up there, talking about goofy things.

But Juvenal said, "In his day. He's still at it, isn't he?''

And Lynn said, "Don't listen to anything he tells you.''

"I already have.''

There, and they were off again. Juvenal got comfortable on the couch with his beer and a bowl of popcorn and told her Bill Hill's plan for nationwide TV exposure, the Juvenal message—*apologia,* Juvenal's word—entering millions of Christian homes. Juvenal grinning as he told it, Lynn not grinning, shaking her head.

"Why not?"

"He's a con artist."

"He's your friend."

"He's still a con artist. You'll end up with nothing."

"He hasn't offered me anything."

"See? You think he's getting you into this for free? He sold them a package and he's making all the money. I know it, because he asked me to be his partner."

"Tell him you'll do it."

"I don't understand you at all," Lynn said. "He's *using* you and you want me to help him."

"He's not *using* me if I let him. I'm agreeing to it."

"Why?"

"Why not?"

"Come on, you don't hide out for years and then decide to go on national television."

"I wasn't hiding, I was doing what I was told. Up to a point. Now I've got a choice," Juvenal said. "All right, here I am. This is what happens to me. This is what I think about it. I'm not ashamed of it, am I? And I'm not self-conscious especially. So why not? I don't make any claims, I don't say I'm an instrument of God . . . even though I might be."

"There," Lynn said. "Though you might be. Tell me something. What do you think about when you heal people?"

"I don't try to think about anything."

"Do you ask God to heal them?"

"No. I feel . . . sad, I guess. I feel sorry for whoever it is."

"Somebody's gonna call up—or Howard Hart, that asshole'll say, 'All right, smart guy. You think you can heal people, why don't you visit hospitals and heal everybody?' "

"I don't say I *think* I can heal people. I say it's happened. That's the whole point. I make no claims, so why would anybody try to shoot me down? From where? I'm here on the ground, I'm a realist, I accept everything that happens. I'm not trying to change the world."

"Maybe you should," Lynn said.

He said, still mildly, almost always mildly, "Make up your mind."

"You get me confused," Lynn said. "I don't have any trouble at all talking to people, communicating, but I get with you, I don't know what to think or what I'm saying sometimes. I'll tell you, it's not like getting your record in the top forty."

"I'm sorry," Juvenal said, "really. We're talking about, what? You're worried about people taking advantage of me. I say, but how can they if I know they're doing it? You're afraid people will challenge me, try to tear down my—what?—my veracity. But how can they if I make no claims?"

"You don't know people. If you rock their boat, their safe beliefs, they'll come after you."

"Then they'll be worrying the same as you are, over nothing. If I disturb people, if they say I'm a fake, a phony, I say, believe what you want. What difference does it make? If they say go to the hospital, buddy, let's see how good you are, I'll go to the hospital. I'll heal people or I won't. Either way, it'll be done. So what's the problem?"

"You make it sound so simple."

"Outside of maybe running out of blood."

"Could that happen?" Like a wide-eyed little girl.

"That's a stigmatic joke. You don't hear too many."

How do you want it? Lynn thought.

Go from the hairdo hotshots to the nice innocent guy and say to yourself perfect, no sham, no bullshit, great— to always know exactly where you are. Except that being close to him was not as simple as it looked. Or maybe it was only simple in principle: to be straightforward, honest; never lie or play roles or pretend or worry or get upset or angry. Only if it was momentary, controlled . . . or for fun, kidding around. Don't think so much, or feed on resentments or hangups. Be you and responsible for you. "You make me mad" was the same as saying, "You make me weigh a hundred and five pounds." The choice was yours. Don't say, "This is awful. Why is it happening to me?" Say, "Why do I think it's awful?" And find out the real reason, not the apparent one. Say, "Why shouldn't it happen to me?" And look at it quietly, objectively. Simple. But not easy. Get rid of years and years of crap cluttering your mind.

Treat serious things seriously, but don't get heavy about it.

She said, "What is it you want to be, a TV star?"

He said, "Well, I've got to do something, and I don't think saints are making it these days. What do you think?"

"No, your saints are a little too low-profile."

"Unless I was a martyr—"

"That's a short run," Lynn said. "How would you like to be a record promoter? I can see you with the Cobras."

"I might like them."

Lynn thought about it. "You know what? You probably would. Or what you could do, you could heal them. Straighten them out." She liked that idea and began to smile, thinking about it, thinking of others then . . . August Murray. She said, "What if you just devoted your life to healing assholes? Turning them into human beings."

They discussed it in serious tones, Lynn supplying names, all kinds of names, and they seemed to be considering it, until the buzzer buzzed. Lynn said they didn't have to answer it; ten to one it was Bill Hill back again. Juvenal said, but if he's here and we're here— Lynn said all right, he can stay fifteen minutes, and buzzed the door, knowing it was Bill Hill. It wasn't.

It was Kathy Worthington with her canvas bag, her note pad, and a flat little GE tape recorder: Kathy here to interview Lynn Faulkner (friend of Juvenal's or what?) and walking into what looked like a typical Somerset hot setup. (If the place wasn't famous for it, at least there was talk.) But even better than that, Juvenal himself was here, involved in popcorn, beer, and, obviously, the little KMA record promoter. Kathy said hi and they said hi.

Kathy said to Juvenal, "You know, I caught your act Sunday and it wasn't bad." Trying to get a rise.

They laughed and she didn't know why, until she became aware of the glances at each other, the grins, and began to feel the off-center, free-form mood, a couple of little kids playing house, or doctor, the barefoot miracle worker and the record promoter with her blouse half open, no bra, both of them subdued but still glowing, trying to suppress the feeling of whatever they had been up to in a dim, comfortable room on a sunny afternoon. It looked like a half-page Sunday feature, Women's Section, if she could get a few admissions rather than weasels or phony indignation.

Kathy took out her tape recorder. They said nothing. She turned it on. They still didn't say anything. She began to ask questions, slipping into her no-bullshit reporter role:

KATHY: Have you known each other long?
JUVIE: We sort of grew up together.

KATHY: You did? Where?

JUVIE: Right here.

KATHY: No, really . . .

LYNN: Isn't he cute? I could eat him up. Actually we've been trying to figure out what he's gonna be. Like what he should do with his, you might say, particular talent.

KATHY: What did you decide?

LYNN: We're thinking he could hang out backstage at rock concerts and heal . . . well, certain performers.

KATHY: Heal them? Of what?

LYNN: I guess you've never met the Cobras.

KATHY: Do you know what she's talking about?

JUVIE: I have no idea.

KATHY: Then what's so funny? No, forget it. Tell me, are you two living together?

LYNN: We're dating.

KATHY: You're serious?

LYNN: Boy, are we.

JUVIE: We're getting married.

LYNN: We are?

JUVIE: Isn't that what you do?

LYNN: I haven't even thought about it.

JUVIE: What've you been doing?

LYNN: I guess when we have time to talk, make some plans. Yeah, why not?

KATHY: You don't think it would be, well, *strange*, being married to a stigmatist? Is it stigmatic or stigmatist?

JUVIE: I think either one.

LYNN: Strange? Are you kidding? But he's really a neat guy. He's kind, considerate . . . absolutely honest. I just hate to think what's gonna happen when he gets on TV.

KATHY: On what, a talk show?

LYNN: On Howard Hart.

KATHY: Oh . . . Do you know what you're getting into?

JUVIE: Is it like Mike Douglas?

KATHY: You mean you've never seen Howard Hart?

JUVIE: I don't think so.

LYNN: The only thing good about it, Howard hasn't seen Juvie either, so they're even.

KATHY: Aren't you being a bit naive? In fact, I was going to ask you anyway . . . Why are you allowing yourself to be used, exploited?

JUVIE: Am I?

KATHY: Are you a traditionalist, a member of August Murray's group?

JUVIE: No, I'm not.

KATHY: Then you're being used.

LYNN: He isn't if he knows it. He *knows* what's going on.

KATHY: Then you have to be awfully naive.

JUVIE: Why does that make you mad?

KATHY: I'm not mad.

JUVIE: You seem upset.

KATHY: Because you're so fucking naive about all this.

JUVIE: Yeah, but why does it make you mad?

KATHY *(pause)*: I don't know.

JUVIE: You like what you're doing? Your work?

KATHY: Not especially.

JUVIE: Then why don't you do something else?

KATHY: I've been with the paper ten years . . .

JUVIE: And you like to write.

KATHY: Yeah, it's what I *do* . . . Let me turn this goddamn thing off.

Silence.

End of tape.

21

When August Murray was a teen-ager he read how Saint Agapitus at age fifteen was brought before the governor of Palestrina, condemned for being a Christian, flogged, placed in a foul dungeon, had hot coals put on his head, boiling water poured over him, his jaw broken, and thrown to the lions. When the lions refused to eat him the governor had a seizure and died on the spot. "Agapitus was finally beheaded, but not before the example of his resolution had converted the tribune Anastasius."

He read about Saint Agatha, who, upon resisting the advances of the governor of Sicily, was arrested on suspicion of being a Christian, had her flesh ripped by iron hooks, her breasts cut off, and was then thrown onto burning coals, "whereupon a violent earthquake shook the town of Catania and the governor, Quintian, fearing the people would rise up, ordered her taken back to prison." (August decided they would have raped her if they hadn't cut her breasts off.)

August could tell you about Calocerus and Parthenius, who were burned alive; Sebastian, shot through with arrows; Victor, Nicephorus, Claudian, Dioscorus, Serapion, and Papias, pounded to death or hacked to pieces; Fabian, Florian, Dismas, of course, Justa and Rufina and Iraneus of Sirmium, all executed; old Nestor, lynched by a mob in Gaza, along with Eusebius, Nesturbus, and Zeno; about ten Theodores or Theodoras who were put to death; the triplets Speusippus, Eleusippus, and Meleusippus, martyred with their grandmother, Leonilla; Gregory the Wonder Worker, also a martyr, who moved mountains, changed the course of rivers, and appointed Alexander the Charcoal Burner, in spite of his rags and dirty face, bishop of Comana in Pontus; and, of course, Chrysogonus, John and Paul, Andrew, Peter, Laurence, Cosmos and Damian and Victor of Marseilles.

It was too bad Saint Augustine was not a martyr. He took a concubine and had a son by her. In fact, from what August could find out, Augustine screwed a lot of women in North Africa before deciding to dedicate his life to Christ. Thereafter he was continually engaged in the defense of the Catholic faith *against schismatics, heretics, and pagans*. He died August 28, 430, ''in a spirit of great courage, humility, and penitence.''

The first important paper August Murray ever wrote was entitled ''What the Church Needs Today Is a Good Persecution.''

The paper wasn't the reason he was kicked out of the seminary; his English teacher, Father Skiffington, agreed with him. But it was an indication of August's problem. He had trouble with rules of conduct, blind discipline, all the no-questions-asked humility shit. He believed the Church needed fighters—anybody could see that—and not the bunch of good little mama's boys the seminary was turning out. It was true that Saint Augustine had died in a spirit of humility (and courage and penitence), but he was seventy-six years old and humility could be a wise move at that age; but not when the Church needed men who weren't afraid to stand up and defend their faith against the cowards within and the Communists without (the sons of bitches).

August transferred to the University of Detroit, majored in sociology, minored in philosophy, and graduated cum laude.

He joined the Catholic Laymen's League, which was dedicated to rooting out Communist fronters from the Church and clergy. But the CLL was never active enough for him. He left to found Outrage, along with the Gray Army of the Holy Ghost (membership, a hundred dollars a year), and began writing and distributing pamphlets. The first one he printed, and still his favorite, was the one about the Church needing a good persecution.

August wasn't afraid to be persecuted. He had demonstrated against demonstrators, commie peace makers, political left-wing cowards, lesbian ERAers, fags of all kinds, marijuana creeps in Ann Arbor, equal housing, the right to work, and what's-his-name, the nigger mayor. He'd been arrested a half dozen times and finally convicted of assault, disrupting a Lenten service at Our Lady of Lasalette in Berkley, sentenced to a year probation and ordered to undergo psychiatric examination, which he ducked and they forgot about. Then a disorderly conduct arrest: distributing political literature within three hundred feet of a church, for which he was fined two hundred dollars by a chickenshit colored judge. And right now he was out on a five-hundred-dollar bond awaiting his jury trial in the assault on the guinea priest, Father Ravioli . . . Navaroli.

The Romans used to take Christians, dip them in tar, and set them afire to light up the Colosseum. They threw them to lions, into boiling oil, crucified, decapitated, stoned, roasted alive, pressed them between boards, and tore them limb from limb. August had been fined two hundred dollars one time, put on probation another.

In a daydream he used to serialize when he was younger—and still imagined from time to time—August was Augustus, a Christian of ancient Rome. He lived in the catacombs at a time when all the Christians were scared to death of getting caught and thrown into the arena, except Augustus. He always carried one of those short swords beneath his toga and made a specialty of avenging martyred Christians. He killed gladiators who killed Christians. He killed the guy who imported the lions. He killed soldiers who raped Christian girls and sold them into slavery. In one of his favorite sequences, Augustus would slip into the villa of a wealthy Roman, free the slaves, and assassinate the master as he lounged in his atrium eating sweetmeats and hummingbirds: see the guy cowering, whimpering, begging for mercy, and drive his sword into the Roman's fat body. One day Augustus would be captured—after killing about twenty of them—and crucified atop one of the seven hills of Rome. He would take three days to die and people would come out from the city to marvel at this heroic martyr with the calm look on his handsome face. (August had always thought it would make a good movie, but could not decide who should play his part.)

He'd be playing himself on television this Saturday, featured on Howard Hart's "Hartline" as Juvenal's closest friend and adviser and . . . maybe suggest to Howard something like, "the Ralph Nader of the Church." ". . . And now I would like to introduce a man I consider the Ralph Nader of the Church, a man whom, no doubt, you have read about in the paper numerous times as the firebrand leader of Outrage, but who possesses, I found in talking to him backstage"— continues Howard Hart—"a cool demeanor and what you might call a razor-sharp analytical mind. I give you the man who has given us Juvenal, Mr. August Murray."

August didn't see why Hart had to have all those other people on: the kid and his mother, the psychiatrist, the priest—that was a lot of bullshit. Unless they were going to be there just in case.

But if he went on first, yes, they could easily keep talking for two hours. Then he could suggest he be brought back on with Juvenal next week, right, and save the standbys for some other time. Otherwise Hart wouldn't even need them.

August had enjoyed talking to Howard Hart on the phone—he had always respected the man—and was looking forward to the meeting and possible videotaping this afternoon. Hart had said they'd tape it unless he decided to go live for phone-in questions, audience participation. August hoped it would be live; there was less chance of getting edited, important words cut out. But he'd play it by ear. He wasn't worried about thinking on his feet, getting into a little give and take, with Hart playing devil's advocate to keep it lively. August was ready.

He'd have to give Bill Hill credit for coming up with the TV idea. It had surprised him at first, the man didn't appear to have the brains of a used car salesman. But by now August had analyzed Bill Hill and had a clear reading: a hanger-on type, one of those people who liked to be seen with celebrities and hang around the edge of the limelight. Fine, as long as he didn't get in the way.

Okay, things to do today, Friday, August 19:

Be at WQRD at 3:00 P.M. sharp.

Call Greg, get about twenty guys from the Gray Army lined up to be in the audience if the show was broadcast live tomorrow night. No armbands, no demonstrating; but with prepared questions in case Hart opened it up to the audience.

Try Juvenal again.

August dialed, sitting at his dad's desk in the print shop, and the snotty colored girl on the desk at Sacred Heart answered. She tried to disguise her accent, but August could tell it was her.

(Had Saint Augustine, before he was a saint, fooled around with colored girls in North Africa?)

"I called all day yesterday and he wasn't there." Like it was the girl's fault.

"And I kept telling you he wasn't, didn't I?"

"Where is he today?"

"He's on his vacation."

"On his vacation? What do you mean he's on his vacation?"

"I *think* I mean he went on a vacation. Isn't that what I said?"

"Where'd he go?"

"Up north somewhere."

"I don't believe you."

"I'll take a polygraph," the girl said, "and send you the results. He's not here, he picked up his suitcase and he's gone."

"When'd he pick it up?"

"I have no idea," the girl said. "There's a little three-by-five card here says, 'Juvie on vacation. Gone up north. Back eight twenty-six.' Now what else can I tell you?" She blinked at the sound of August hanging up his receiver and added, under her breath, "Motherfucker."

It was annoying, agonizing, frustrating . . . infuriating—he'd get the right word—to try to do something intrinsically meaningful and have a bunch of mindless . . . pretentious people always in the way . . .

Thinking this as he went to the front door of the shop, opened it, and picked up the Friday morning *Free Press*.

Thinking, he had to get Juvenal away from everybody, under wraps, so he could prepare him, condition him, get him in the right frame of mind . . . as he brought the paper back to the desk, glanced at the front page, turned it and saw, jumping out at him from page 3, Juvenal and the girl, the *girl,* grinning at each other like two little kids above the headline:

Says the Woman in Juvie's Life:
"He's Really a Neat Guy . . ."
By Kathy Worthington
Free Press staff writer

"Isn't he cute?" said Lynn. "I could eat him up." Don't be surprised at anything you read these days. Neither Lynn nor Juvenal is the least bit bashful on the subject of love and their intention to marry "once we have time to talk about it and make plans."

Charlie Juvenal Lawson is the former Franciscan brother who, day by day, gains more national notoriety as mystic faith healer and the world's only known stigmatic. Or is it stigmatist? "Either is accepted," said Juvie.

"Oh, God—" August groaned. And missed what Kathy wrote about Juvie's boyish charm belying his ability to empathize, a gift that appeared to border on extrasensory perception. August missed it as his eyes dropped like a stone to:

"Lynn Faulkner, who makes her home in fashionable Somerset Park, digs cranberry crushed velvet, chrome and Waylon Jennings, *was* a career-minded pop-record promoter, until she met Juvie. "He's really a neat guy," said Lynn, "kind, considerate . . ."

"*Noooooooooooooooo!*" August shrieked. "*God! What are you doing to me!*"
He crushed the section of the newspaper together, squeezing, squeezing with all his strength to compress it into a ball, a limp rag of paper. Then stopped and sat absolutely still, staring at the venetian blinds on the front window, hearing the faint sound of morning traffic. He began to open the ball of paper, flattening it on the desk,

trying to smooth out the creases, looking for page 3 again
and the picture . . .

There.

Lynn Faulkner . . . fashionable Somerset Park. What
did she do to him?

Put something in his coffee, some kind of drug.

Paraded naked in front of him.

Enticed him, lured him, appealed to his libido . . .
ambushed him! Assaulted his purity! Seduced him!
Dragged him down to her depths!

"God, please help me," August prayed, not in a toga
now, not with one of those short Roman swords either.
No, with something way better than a sword right in the
desk drawer. His dad's .38 caliber Smith and Wesson
Commando.

22

Twenty-two fifty-seven Golfview. There it was, *Faulkner*, the fourth name; upstairs. August rang. There was no response.

No one on the street or the walks leading up to the cluster of apartment buildings. Everybody away or at work or in out of the sun. He walked around to the back—or the front of the building, whichever it was— where two cement-slab patios and two balconies above looked out on the golf course and two people way off on another fairway. One balcony stripped, empty, the people obviously away. So it wasn't hers.

The other balcony was hers, with the porch furniture, August reasoned, because he *knew* the colored girl had lied to him. Juvenal wasn't away on vacation, he was being seduced by the little blond cunt who wasn't answering her doorbell and was up there right now "maneuvering, manipulating, contaminating him with her body, shoving it in his face"—lines for a pamphlet— "draining his will, which was innocent, unsuspecting, and tragically, treacherously"—check *The Word Finder*— "weakened or sapped by the determined thrusting of her sex at him." Or, "the relentless thrusting."

It would never occur to August that he was sometimes dumb-lucky, that he made the right move for the wrong reason. Half right, anyway. Yes, it was Lynn's apartment. But no, there was nobody home.

To find it out he took two metal chairs from the downstairs patio, piled one on top of the other, tested them, climbed up, caught the toe of his goddamn sandal in a chair rung, fell with the chairs and hit his forehead on the cement; climbed up again, reached the balcony railing, and pulled himself over—not wasting any time now—wanting to punch a hole in the glass door with his gun butt, Christ, and shattered the whole pane, hunching his shoulders at the sound, but it was done; he slid the door open and rushed through the apartment to the bedroom, revolver ready, like he was raiding a whorehouse.

Shit.

He stood there looking around.

August had never been in a girl's apartment before. It was quiet. He felt strange. He wondered what was in here, if she had sexual objects, picturing a garter belt and a black vibrator. He began opening drawers. He looked at her panties. He looked at a box of Tampons and read the directions. He looked at bras that were so flimsy he could hold them up and see light through the cups. He found a little enema behind the bathroom door; good, she was constipated. There were jars and tubes in the bathroom bearing names like Elancyl and Ethera, which August believed were applied, somehow, to female reproductive organs, but he didn't find a garter belt or a vibrator. He went out to the front room and looked at Waylon Jennings, studying the giant face, having no idea who it was. August wanted to do something to that face. Mess it up, throw something on it. But what? His hand came up and rested on the row of pens and Magic Markers in his shirt pocket.

"There's more about Elvis," Lynn said. Then, after a few minutes, she said, "Oh, my God."

Juvie opened his eyes—''What's the matter?''—and
raised his head from the towel, seeing a glare of sky and
sand and the high dunes of Sleeping Bear way off where
the beach curved out into Lake Michigan . . . and Lynn
in the yellow bikini sitting cross-legged on a towel. She
was looking down at the newspaper on her lap, the
Chicago Tribune, holding one temple of her sunglasses so
they wouldn't slip off.

''Something terrible happened to Waylon.''

''What?''

''Poor guy. He was picked up on a dope charge. Coke.
I guess possession.''

''Oh.'' Juvie lowered his head and closed his eyes
again.

''Yeah, possession,'' Lynn said. ''One gram, that's all.
They arrested him in Nashville.''

''Is that a lot, a gram?''

''Hardly more than a small party, depending who your
friends are. He could get fifteen years and a fifteen-
thousand-dollar fine. God, one gram.''

''Do you use it?''

''I have, but I wouldn't go out of my way for it. It's
okay,'' Lynn said. ''But listen, you know what I'd like
to do? I mean when we have time. Go down to Luckenback, Texas.''

''Okay.'' Juvie's eyes remained closed. He wore red
swimming trunks and a glaze of suntan lotion.

''You know where I mean?''

''In the song,'' Juvie said. ''What's there?''

''Nothing, really.''

''Then what do you want to go for?''

''It's got one fireplug, one store, two houses, a shade
tree, and a lot of cold beer, and you know what? Everybody's going there to see it on account of Waylon's song
. . . to get back to the basics of life. If it was spring we
could go down for Mud Dauber Day. It's an annual

event; people go down there and drink beer and wait for
the first mud dauber wasps to show up. But you know
what? I like 'If You See Me Getting Smaller' better than
'Luckenback, Texas.' "

"I like 'Lucille' . . . in a bar in Toledo," Juvie said.
"The place I'd like to see is Nashville."

"You ain't ever been to Nashville?" Lynn would get
more down-home at the mention of it. "I'll tell you what.
We go Interstate 65 to Nashville, turn right, head over to
Texas and pick up 35 south to Austin and it's eighty miles
to Luckenback."

"You've been there?"

"Uh-unh, but I know the way."

They ate smoked chub they bought on the dock in
Leland where the fishing boats came in . . . went for a
thrill ride in a dune scooter, a trip across the Sahara on
the shores of Lake Michigan . . . returned to the motel
and made love in the afternoon and slept in each other's
arms, it was so good.

Look at it now, calmly, Lynn thought. Why *should* it
end?

She read their horoscopes in *Town & Country* and felt
encouraged; read his first, Aquarius, aloud, beginning
with, " 'Saturn has put you through the mill the last
couple of years . . .' "

He said, "*That's* who it was."

" '. . . but it has also in some way refined you. So
what you experience this month may be no more than a
total and final truth session.' Neat? 'You also enter a
completely different phase in your career now and over
the next few months.' Really, I'm not making it up, that's
what it says." There were also references to "matters of
a partnership nature" and deciding "whether or not the
bonds are strong enough to hold a relationship together."

"Are they?"

"They're awful strong," he said.

That was good because Lynn, a Libra, wasn't going to "have much time for friendships and close involvements," she'd be "preoccupied with your career."

"What do they know?" Lynn said. "But wait. 'The New Moon on the fourteenth'—that was last Sunday—'heralds an entirely new chapter and one in which you will want and certainly be required to present quite a different face to the world.' Now that part's true, isn't it?" Lynn said. "I just read it for fun, I don't believe in it. But every once in a while it comes pretty close; like a new beginning on the fourteenth, that's certainly true. *Town & Country* and *Cosmopolitan* are the best. The ones in the paper, I think they make them up." She paused. "Are you okay?"

"I'm fine."

"Are you sad?"

"Maybe; I don't know."

"It's all right to be sad," Lynn said. "There are sad things." She waited a moment, lying on the messed-up twin bed with the magazine, Juvenal on the made-up twin after popping open cans of beer and lying down there to listen to their horoscopes.

"Are you thinking about the little boy on the beach?"

"I was."

The boy, about six years old, with withered stick legs, had been with his family, his two sisters, his mother and father, at a campsite of beach chairs, blanket, picnic basket, rubber rafts. His father had carried him down to the water and held him while the boy waved his arms, screaming happily, and splashed and pretended to swim . . . Juvenal sitting on his towel watching them.

"You can't just . . . heal everybody, can you?"

"I don't know."

"Did anybody ask Padre Pio, you mentioned, or any of the saints that healed people?"

"Ask them what?"

"If they could heal everybody."

"Not that I know of."

"What you said before—doesn't the person have to feel something? Like want to be healed?"

"I don't know. I thought so, but I'm not sure."

"Did you want to? I mean with the boy today."

"Yes. But I was afraid it wouldn't happen, I wouldn't be able to."

"Have you been afraid before?"

"No. In the times before I never thought about it. It just happened," Juvenal said. "Except in church last Sunday I was beginning to think about it—I remember now—and be afraid, with the children coming up the aisle. What was gonna happen? What was I supposed to do? But then the boy ran up to me."

Lynn waited again. "You're not responsible for everybody."

He didn't say anything.

"Do you think you are?"

"No. I mean I don't know. Tell me what I *am* responsible for."

She said, "It isn't something you can think about, is it? Or you can't say, if I'm this . . . if I'm a house painter I should paint houses, it's what I'm supposed to do. It isn't like that, is it?"

"No," he said, "it isn't clear. It seems to be, but it isn't." He was silent a moment. "I grope, feel my way along."

"Who's being dramatic now?" Lynn said.

He looked over at her and seemed to smile; but it was like someone trying to hide grief or pain. "A time comes every so often, I say to myself, why me?"

"Like the little boy on the beach will say to himself one day," Lynn said.

He kept looking at her with the expression of concealed

grief until she came over to his bed to lie close to him and hold him.

"I need you," Juvenal said.

Howard Hart spoke to a man from Garden City who had been a few years older than Elvis when they were both growing up in Tupelo, Mississippi. The man said Elvis was always following the older boys around and they'd have to yell at him to go on home. "He was just a snot-nosed regular boy," the man from Garden City said.

Howard was told by an educator from Bob Jones University, Greenville, South Carolina, that Elvis was "morally debauched" and contributed to the ruin of America's moral fiber and the breakdown of the family unit. Howard asked the educator if he'd say that on the air.

He read in the paper about Elvis pulling a gun and shooting out his TV set the time Robert Goulet was singing, as described by one of Elvis's bodyguards. Howard told his secretary to see if she could reach the bodyguard by phone.

He spoke to a girl who said her name was Peggy Chavez and claimed to be Elvis's real girl friend and not that Ginger somebody who was supposed to have found him dead. Peggy said, "Sure, I was with him plenty times in Vegas and L.A." Howard wondered if it was the same girl who once claimed to have been with Ozzie Nelson plenty times in Bakersfield.

It didn't matter. He invited the boyhood friend from Garden City, the educator, and the girl friend—he couldn't reach the bodyguard—to be on the program this Saturday, Howard Hart's Elvis Presley Memorial Show, and had his secretary go out and tell the "miracle crowd" waiting in the lobby he'd get back to them in a couple of weeks.

* * *

The psychiatrist said, "Don't call us, we'll call you, uh? What's he got, some hermaphrodites? Forget it." He walked out. The hematologist and the theologian sat there not knowing what to do, the theologian lighting another cigarette. Bill Hill said, well, they could go over to the Perfect Blend and have a two-for-one happy hour drink. Antoinette Baker said fine with her. August Murray, tense, said he was going to "get some straight answers out of Howard Hart if he had to break the man's arm, or worse."

Bill Hill and Antoinette were on their second round of dry Manhattans, four for the price of two, when August walked in, sat down with them in the empty side of the booth, and ordered a ginger ale.

Bill Hill said, "No luck?"

"They tried to keep me out," August said. "I went in his office, looked around the studio; he wasn't there."

"I meant to ask you," Bill Hill said, "what you did to your head."

"I bumped it."

"That's a mean-looking bruise."

"Poor Richie," Antoinette Baker said. "Everybody's calling him fuzz-head now, the other kids. I told him"—pouting as she said it—"don't you pay any attention to the little shitbirds."

She was a stylish woman and she smelled nice, had on turquoise Navajo earrings and a low V to her white dress, giving Bill Hill a glimpse of healthy breasts with little blue veins. She wore her nails long, polished a deep red, and a big turquoise ring, the hand holding a cigarette and tapping off the ash every few seconds. She had told them Richie was back "on the ward" again, but just for observation. That's why she hadn't brought him. He was healed, she knew it; and he'd be fine on the TV program if they ever went on the air. She said she had told Richie to just act natural and say yes, sir, and no, sir, which he would because he was a little gentleman. But it sure pissed him off when the kids called him fuzz-head.

Antoinette talked a lot, but was not hard to steer, Bill Hill found. He had been suggesting he could contact the *National Enquirer* for her. Maybe she'd like to sell them a copyrighted interview as the working mother of a boy miraculously healed. But he didn't want to talk about it in front of August, who sat hunched over the table holding onto his glass of ginger ale—in case anyone were to come up and try to grab it away from him. Dumb shit. He was going to get round-shouldered. Down there stewing, smoldering, instead of holding his head up, alert to opportunity; yes, and all kinds of young happy hour secretaries coming into the place now, eyeing the young hotshots in their three-piece business suits.

He said to August, "There's a lot of talent around, if you're interested."

August looked past his shoulder at the secretaries; he didn't say anything.

Antoinette said, "I was really surprised to read about Juvenal and his girl friend. That kinda surprised the hell out of me. I mean a holy person—you don't, you know, think of them making out or even being interested in girls. He was very nice and Richie liked him a lot—"

"I guess he would," Bill Hill said.

"—but he didn't strike me as being that way, you know, even though you read about priests all the time now running off with nuns"—flicking ashes—"which is fine, I mean I'm not gonna judge or condemn anybody as long as they're not hurting other people."

Bill Hill let her talk, because he wasn't sure if he wanted to discuss Lynn and Juvenal. If he decided he didn't, he'd switch Antoinette onto something else, like herself, which was a foolproof way to switch a person.

What did Bill Hill think of the new Lynn and Juvenal, as reported by Kathy Worthington? Well, at first he hit a

ceiling inside his head and wanted to storm over to
Somerset and shake Lynn and tell her, "Look, for God
sake, at what you're doing to a holy instrument of the
Lord." Or, "Well, what's it like knowing you've fucked
up a young man's entire life?" On the other hand, after
calming down and looking at it again, he could say to
her, grinning, "You son of a gun. You . . . son . . . of
. . . a . . . gun." Bill Hill could go either way. And the
more he thought about it, the more he was convinced he
should ride with it. *Ride* with it? Hell, drive it home.
Face the realities of life with neither fear nor loathing and
you'll come out ahead. Nothing was ever as bad as it
seemed. You could go to a man like Howard Hart, after
he came out of hiding in the toilet from August, and say,
"Well, how do you like the setup now? You get not only
a miracle-working faith healer, but one that's in love and
living with a popular young Detroit record promoter. Now
then, how'd you also like to have on your show—"

"What's her name?" Antoinette said. "Lynn
something?"

"—Lynn Marie Faulkner," Bill Hill said. "Sweet little
girl used to work for me. We've been close friends eleven
and a half years."

"I think it's real cute," Antoinette said. "A man like
that *should*, you know, get out more and find out what
life's all about. I'm a Catholic, went to Catholic schools
and all—"

"You mean you *were* a Catholic," August said.
"Maybe when you were little."

"I still am. I was baptized one."

"You go to mass on Sunday?"

"Sometimes."

"You make your Easter duty?"

"God, I haven't heard that in years."

"You dance naked in a beer garden and you say you're
a Catholic?"

"*Beer* garden?" Antoinette said.

"That's one I haven't heard in years," Bill Hill said. "I believe they're all lounges now."

August said, "You say you're a friend of hers, but you didn't speak to her?" When Bill Hill looked at him he said, "I'm talking about Lynn, or whatever her name is." Like August didn't want to say the name aloud or even think it. "Where is she?"

Bill Hill said, "What do you mean, where is she?"

"She isn't home. She must've gone somewhere with Juvenal."

"I think that's nice," Antoinette said. "Get off by themselves. I was going to say, being a Catholic—"

"You're *not* a Catholic," August said. He couldn't let it go.

"*Being* a Catholic," Antoinette said, "I've always thought that priests, that people would listen to priests more if they had a little experience instead of talking about sex and marriage and things and not knowing a goddamn thing about it—"

August said, "You don't have to jump in mud to know it gets you dirty."

"I knew you were gonna say that," Antoinette said. "That's exactly the kind of reasoning they use on you; fucking priests, you know why they join up? Because they're afraid of women."

"And you're gonna tell me you're a *Cath*olic?"

Bill Hill let them argue, thinking about Lynn and Juvenal. If they had gone off together, this was the first he'd heard of it. It was a job managing people, trying to keep them from messing up or wasting their talent; hoping Lynn wasn't right now nibbling on Juvie's ear and telling him he shouldn't be on TV. He wished there were more Antoinettes and fewer Augusts getting in the way, August sitting there with a fiery cross up his ass. What did anybody need August for?

The man was easy to dislike. You wanted to pick at him, gang up on him. Probably he'd had the same effect on other kids when he was little, being a born asshole, so that ducking rocks and getting depantsed and his face washed with dirty snow had turned him into the beauty he was today, with his tight ass and all his pencils.

Bill Hill said, "August, excuse me. What do you do for fun?"

"I work," August said. "What do you think I do?"

"I just wondered," Bill Hill said. "I'd like to watch you demonstrate sometime. You got any good demonstrations coming up?"

"When we demonstrate," August said, "you'll hear about it."

He was hard to antagonize because he was so dumb and didn't have a sense of humor. Bill Hill said to him, "Can I ask you a personal question?"

"What?" Sullen and guarded.

"How come you aren't married?"

"How come *you* aren't?" August said.

"I had a lovely wife, Barbararose, and her memory is all I can handle. Really, how come you aren't?"

"I haven't had time for anything like that," August said.

"Women, I imagine though, are attracted to you."

"Jesus," Antoinette said.

August gave her his cold killer look and Bill Hill said, "I'm serious. Don't you get a certain number of women attracted to your cause?"

"We don't allow women in Outrage," August said. "You have priests and you have nuns; we have our organization and the women have the Daughters of the Holy Ghost Society."

"With a silent 'h,' " Antoinette said, having a good time. "The D-O-G-S."

She wasn't bad, Bill Hill had to admit; he'd have to tell her so later.

Right now Antoinette was saying, "That's the whole goddamn trouble in the Catholic Church, all that boy-girl shit, keeping them separated so they won't have impure thoughts and get aroused. You ever get aroused, August? Come on by the club sometime and we'll check you out."

August was being cool now; he gave her a look and finished his ginger ale without saying anything.

Yes, she was quick all right. Bill Hill was thinking he might check her out himself, see the professional side of Richie's mom. He liked friendly, open women who wore perfume and Navajo jewelry.

August had taken a handful of coins out of his pocket and was selecting some of them. He was a dumb shit and there was nothing anyone could do about it. Bill Hill said, "I got it, August. Put your money away." He did, without any insisting. Bill Hill looked at his watch. "Well, if you don't have any demonstrations planned—"

"I've got something I'm gonna do," August said.

"Is that right? Whereabouts?"

"You'll read about it."

"You mean we can't watch?"

"You'll read about it," August said, "and you'll remember we sat here talking while you and"—he looked at Antoinette—"this one were making all these clever remarks, trying to put me on. You know what you were doing and so do I. But just remember one thing. I warned you."

"About what?" Bill Hill said. "You haven't told us anything."

"I told you you'll read about it," August said, pausing as he slid out of the booth. "And there won't be a thing you'll be able to do to me, either."

"Like what?" Bill Hill said. "August?"

But August was walking away.

Bill Hill watched him. "He doesn't make any sense."

"Because he's a little shitbird," Antoinette said.

Days later, six days, their last day on the beach near Glen Arbor, Michigan, south of Leland, Lynn said, "Have you decided, definitely?"

"Yeah, I'm gonna do it."

"You're sure?"

"Why're you so nervous?"

"Because I've seen his program. He's a rotten guy. He'll deliberately try to make you look bad."

"Not if I don't make any claims," Juvie said. "Who me? Look him right in the eye and keep the facts straight. Why shouldn't it work out?"

"Like the write-up in *Time*."

"That wasn't so bad."

There were copies of *Time* and *Newsweek* in Lynn's straw bag with straight-fact stories about Juvenal. *Time* described him as "the boyish missionary out of Brazil with the sometime gift of grabbing children with crippling diseases, turning on with the stigmata and performing a sanguine healing rite that leaves Juvenal emotionally drained and the children, according to eyewitnesses, jumping for joy. Not since Padre Pio . . ." And speculation as to whether or not he had the makings of a saint. There was no mention of the fact the would-be saint had a girl friend.

Juvenal had called the Center the day before to let them know he'd be back in town Friday. There were messages waiting from local television stations, from the *National Enquirer, Midnight, People,* and *Us*. Lynn told him to wait till *Family Circle* got in touch.

She said, "What're we going back to? Are you starting to get an idea?"

He said, "I told them I'd be on the program, otherwise

we wouldn't even have to go. We're not committed to do anything we don't want to.''

She was hesitant watching him closely, waiting for the catch. ''What do we do after that?''

''Whatever you want.''

''We don't even have to live in Detroit, do we?''

He said, ''No, we could move to Cleveland if we want.''

They stared at each other, straight-faced. She said, ''Or East St. Louis.''

He said, ''What would you think of Gary, Indiana?''

''Akron,'' Lynn said.

''Rock Island?''

''Where's that?''

''Right next to Moline.''

''How about Canton, Ohio?''

''Calumet City.''

''Dubuque.''

He said, ''What's the matter with Dubuque?''

When they were in the motel room for the last time, packing to leave, she said, ''We actually can live anywhere we want, can't we?''

''Anywhere,'' he said.

She waited for him to say, ''But,'' or ''Except that,'' or put it off by saying, ''We don't have to talk about it right now''—but he didn't. So whatever it was that would mess them up would have to come from the outside. Something waiting at home. Something hidden in all he was involved in. A legal or ecclesiastical voice saying, ''Oh, no, you don't. Forget it.''

She said, ''You could grow a beard.''

''Yeah, I guess I could.''

''We could change our names.''

''How about Lynn Lawson?''

See? It was simple, right there, nothing to force. He held her and looked at her, she could *see* he loved her.

There was enough love between them—it was spilling over, giving her a good feeling about everyone she met and all the people she knew; good old Bill Hill . . . even August Murray didn't seem so bad. She kept saying to herself, in sort of a semiprayer, If it's good, then it should happen. If God wants us to be good and also wants us to be happy, then . . . and then the words in her mind, the reasoning, would go around in circles though the meaning to her was clear. If God didn't want them to make it, then He wouldn't have let them get this far. Otherwise it wouldn't be fair. And if God wasn't fair then there was no reason to believe in Him.

Juvie said, "What does God have to do with it?"

She said, "He knows everything that's gonna happen, doesn't He?"

Juvie said, "Knowing isn't causing."

Strange. For a man so close to God he didn't sound very religious. But it wasn't something to worry about. There was *nothing* to worry about, nothing specific that she could picture. He'd appear on television, answer all questions, be insulted and misquoted—there, that would be done. They'd stay on the move until the publicity died off and then get married at downtown Saint Mary's . . . stay in Detroit and keep their jobs, or . . .

On the way home, she said, "We don't have to be poor, do we? Like in poor but honest?" Thinking, God, I hope not.

He said, "No. Why should we be poor?"

For a moment she saw herself in an inner-city ghetto mission, a repainted and repainted storefront place with a high tin ceiling and a lot of old black people lined up to get something.

She said, "You know, I wasn't kidding. I think you'd make a really good record promoter."

23

Each afternoon August Murray returned to Lynn's apartment, picked up the paper in the upstairs hall, let himself in with the extra key he'd found in the kitchen, and dropped the paper on the growing pile of morning editions on the coffee table. If she hadn't stopped delivery, August reasoned, they wouldn't be gone long; maybe a few days.

On the second visit he was going to pick up the broken glass all over the carpeting, but changed his mind. He'd leave it to look like the work of the burglar who came in, was surprised by the girl . . .

Sometimes he would see people on the golf course, but never anyone close by or coming into the building. If he was ever stopped and questioned, he was her brother, checking on the place while she was gone.

On the third visit he found a pair of men's undershorts and the shavecoat. He looked around again thoroughly during the next visits but didn't find anything else incriminating or any sexual objects; though he was sure—sitting in the living room looking around, thinking of places—there were sexual objects in the apartment somewhere. "I know!" he said to himself one time, jumped up and went to the kitchen to look in the refrigerator, thinking that maybe some sexual objects had to be stored in a cold place. There wasn't much in the refrigerator: a nearly empty bottle of wine, one can of beer, milk, yogurt, wilted celery and carrot sticks, Cool Whip . . . *Cool Whip*. Maybe.

He waited every afternoon and into the evening from August 20 to August 26, a few times returning a little later, around midnight, to check the apartment from the golf course side, see if there was a light on.

Waiting in an apartment . . . waiting in a Roman villa, gun instead of a short sword. There was little difference. The purpose, the intent, was the main thing.

He rehearsed it and pictured it.

The girl comes in, stops, surprised to see him sitting in the chair. "What do you want? What are you doing here?" Juvenal, if he was with her, would say something in that lethargic way of his—which could be a result of his bleeding so much, a chronic weakness associated with stigmata.

It didn't make sense that someone like Juvenal, who seemed so indifferent, so wishy-washy about it, would be given the stigmata when, Christ, if August had it he'd know exactly what to do. First he'd vow, unequivocally, it was an act of God and describe apparitions and quote voices he heard during his passion. He would use the stigmata as a stamp of divine approval on the movement to restore traditional rites "as God expects." And he would specialize in healing crippling, nationally recognized diseases and overnight become a bigger name than Albert Schweitzer and Jerry Lewis combined.

If Juvenal was with her he'd tell him to stand aside. If Juvenal tried to say anything, he'd tell him, "Stay out of it!" Then, calmly, "You've been contaminated. As you rid the cripple of his disease, I rid you of yours."

Then shoot her.

Take Juvenal out to Almont and keep him in the rectory. Talk to him, quietly, rationally, with indisputable arguments to justify the removal of a malignant member.

Juvenal would gradually, passively begin to understand and ultimately accept the inevitability of the girl's death. "My friend, as God is my witness, I had no choice." Juvenal would nod docilely and accept, because he seemed to be a better accepter than anything else.

But it didn't work that way. On Friday, the twenty-sixth, August had to wait for a shipment of paper stock. He called the plant, threatened, railed, but still had to wait; so that by the time he got in his Charger and headed for Troy and the Somerset Park Apartments, Lynn and Juvenal were already there.

Lynn saw the newspapers on the coffee table first. Then the broken glass. Then Waylon, with the word *Outrage* written across his face in red Magic Marker, gone over again and again, the word scribbled on in a tasteless lack of style and composition. She did think that for a moment; if somebody—not somebody, *he*, August—was going to mess up Waylon, he could have tried a little harder to make it look good. The guy had no class at all. He broke in—for what?

"Our friend August," Lynn said. "Do you believe it? I don't know why, he reminds me of Toby and Abbott, guys I told you about with the Cobras? They get a bug up their ass they have to wreck something."

Juvenal stood holding the suitcases; he looked from Waylon to the shattered glass door and back again before putting the bags down.

Lynn pushed pieces of glass out of the way with her foot. The door frame had been slid aside, the screen door in place. She opened it, went out on the balcony, and stood there. Looking over the rail she said, "The people downstairs go away all the time. All these people living here, but you don't see anybody." After a few moments she came back in. "You ever live in an apartment?"

Juvenal shook his head.

"It's like living way off by yourself," Lynn said. "What would he have against Waylon, for God sake?"

When she walked out of the living room to the hall, Juvenal took the suitcases into the bedroom. Lynn looked in her office, then came through the bedroom to the bath. "I don't know, a few things're out of place. I can see him nosing around. The guy's really weird."

"I guess he is," Juvenal said, sounding resigned. "Did he take anything?"

"Probably my panties," Lynn said. "He looks like a guy who'd be into girls' panties."

August had a feeling they were both here; but at first, opening the door quietly and looking into the living room from the hall, he saw only Lynn and thought, Perfect. Because she was on the floor with newspapers spread all around her, sitting with her back to him . . .

August reached inside his light poplin jacket and drew the .38 Commando from his belt.

. . . and when he shot her she would fall on the newspapers and it would be neater that way. There were scissors on the coffee table, stories with pictures she had cut out of the papers, narrow newsprint columns hanging over the chrome edge of the table.

August raised the revolver and aimed at her short blond hair. He wanted to say something to her, wanted her to see it, but was afraid if she did she might scream and try to run and then the newspapers on the floor wouldn't do any good. He could see her bare knees and thighs; she was wearing a short little sleeveless sundress or something, the hem pushed up and bunched between her brown thighs because of the way she was sitting, cross-legged, hunched over the papers.

She said, "Listen to this," and August jumped. " 'It occurs at first glance these two could be sister and brother, the resemblance is that striking . . .' Did you know we look alike?''

August glanced toward the kitchen, the opening above the counter.

'' 'But any suspicion of kinship is forgotten immediately once you see the way they talk to each other with ''inside'' straight-faced remarks, and notice their lingering looks and glances.' Did you know we did that?''

''I didn't think anyone noticed,'' Juvenal said from the kitchen.

August looked that way again, then back to Lynn. He saw the glass had been picked up.

''You want mustard?''

''A little,'' Lynn said.

''The lettuce isn't any good.''

''Just mustard's fine.''

August listened to it: Juvenal in the kitchen; she sits on her ass letting him wait on her, because she can make him do anything she wants. Raises up her dress and makes him do things.

Juvenal came in from the kitchen carrying a plate of sandwiches and a bowl of potato chips.

He stopped. After a moment he said to August, ''What you have there, that's more than disturbing the peace, even if you're kidding.''

''I'm not kidding,'' August said.

Lynn said, ''Oh, my God,'' looking around, and August swung the gun back to her, seeing her scrambling to her feet. He yelled, ''Don't move!'' But too late. She was standing, holding her hands against her thighs. Now Juvenal was moving.

August swung the revolver on him, not wanting to but had to. ''Stay where you are!'' They were too far apart; yet he didn't want them close together.

Juvenal placed the sandwiches and potato chips on the

counter and walked past August, not looking at him, to Lynn and said something to her—August unable to hear the words—and put his hand on her shoulder. It was easier to cover them, but they were too close together, standing by the glass coffee table. August could see her falling, smashing the table, and began to think, What's wrong with that? In fact, good, smash it. Found in broken glass in a pool of blood— A burglar, someone caught in her apartment, killing her spontaneously, wouldn't worry about being neat.

Juvenal said, "August?"

August said, "You don't have to explain anything to me. I know what's going on, I can see what she's doing to you."

Juvenal said, "All right," showing August he was calm and relaxed so August would be calm and relaxed. "Tell me what you have in mind?"

A question along the line of questions August had anticipated. He had rehearsed several replies, but liked his first one as well as "Rid your life of a malignancy," or any of the others. He said, "I'm gonna get her out of the way once and for all." Plain and simple.

Lynn said, "Out of the way? Out of whose way?"

"His," August said.

"How am I in his way? He can do anything he wants."

Juvenal said, "August, I think you've got a mistaken idea about what's going on. We haven't done anything wrong. Or else I'd realize it, wouldn't I?"

"You've examined your conscience?" August said. "I doubt it. I don't see how you could as long as you remain in an occasion of sin. It's impossible."

"That's what I mean," Juvenal said. "We're talking about *my* conscience, aren't we?"

"Not hers," August said. "She's past having a conscience."

"Well, just to keep it simple," Juvenal said, "if we're talking about mine, then let me say, let me assure you my conscience is in good shape and isn't trying to beat on me or tell me anything."

"That's what happens," August said. "Ignore your conscience and after a while it ceases to function and you're cut off from your moral guidelines. I've seen it happen, a good, scrupulous conscience becoming lax, then losing every bit of its fiber and finally it becomes limp, worthless."

"For Christ sake," Lynn said, "why don't you think I have a conscience?"

"You don't," August said. "You're . . . hollow, without a spark of spiritual life left in you."

"How do *you* know?"

"You can protest all you want, it won't do you any good. But what you're looking at now is the summation and conclusion of your life." He extended the revolver. "*This* is what it's added up to."

"Jesus, August, come on," Lynn said. She felt helpless and wasn't even sure she understood what August was talking about. She said to Juvenal, "Tell him we're okay. We're really nice and we're not doing anything bad. Christ—"

Juvenal said to him, "You're talking ethics with a gun in your hand. You realize that?"

"I certainly do," August said. "We can talk about it later. I'm taking you up to Almont for a few days of recollection; a retreat, you might say. You can talk to Father Nestor or myself, or not speak at all if you feel silence, contemplation, might be better. I'll give you some pamphlets."

Juvenal said, "August, why don't we sit down and talk now?"

"After, we can talk all you want."

Juvenal started toward him. "Put the gun down, okay?"

August backed up a step. "You have nothing to do with this; stay out of it."

Juvenal continued toward him. "If I weren't here, you wouldn't be either."

August moved back again. "You have nothing to do with *this*, right now. Your time's coming and we'll prepare for it."

Juvenal, stepping toward him, almost within reach, said, "Let me have the gun, August. Okay?"

August moved back again and stopped as his left shoulder bumped against the edge of the sliding door. He put the gun on Juvenal, aiming point-blank at his chest.

Lynn said, "August, for God sake, give him the fucking gun, will you?"

She saw August past Juvenal, part of him; saw him look toward her and then at Juvenal and then saw him push Juvenal hard with his left hand and swing the gun toward her in the moment that he was able to aim directly at her.

And fired—the noise, the awful sound ringing close in the room—and fired again and fired again, the third shot into the ceiling as Juvenal came in under August's arm, raising it with one hand, grabbing August's collar in his fist and twisting the fist into August's throat as he rushed him backward onto the balcony, drove him against the rail and over the rail, arms and then legs in the air, August screaming, and then gone.

Lynn could still hear the ringing, her eyes on Juvenal. His back was to her, hands on the iron railing, looking down. When he didn't turn she went out to him and stood close, taking his arm and pressing her body against his hip.

"He hasn't moved," Juvenal said.

She looked over the railing to see August lying at the

edge of the cement-slab patio below. Two metal porch chairs, tipped over, were on either side of him where he lay on his back, arms spread above his head, as if looking up at them with a gesture of surrender.

Juvenal said, "I think I killed him."

24

Howard Hart spoke for twelve minutes on chicanery, legerdemain, apparent miracles, oracles, sensitives, Lourdes, Fatima, faith healing, bending spoons, Uri Geller, the old Oral Roberts, God—using the words *psychogenesis, psycho-biological, psycho-physiological, psychosomatic,* almost every *psych* but *psychedelic* to give his remarks little rings of authority; though none of it made much sense to anyone listening for a topic sentence.

There was a packed house of more than 150 people in the studio audience, including the "miracle crowd" sitting down front: Lynn Faulkner and Bill Hill; Antoinette Baker and Richie's doctor from Children's Hospital (where Richie was still under observation and, Antoinette hoped, watching on TV); Kathy Worthington and Kathy's theology expert from U of D, Father Dillon; Dr. Kaplan, author of *Psychoanalysis: Trick or Treatment;* twenty-seven young men from the Gray Army of the Holy Ghost, in white shirts but without armbands; Father Nestor, sitting in the last row, on the aisle; about forty parishioners from Saint John Bosco; and the rest, fans of "Hartline," sitting, standing, extending out into the WQRD hallway and lobby.

All those people in the studio audience and "all you out there" watching Howard Hart rub the side of his nose and talk about psycho-hyphenated things, half of Howard showing behind the giant Mediterranean desk—bookshelves in the background—the buttoned-up top half in double-breasted silk and big Windsor; the nationally televised star acting natural, caressing the side of his nose, touching his hairpiece. Look at the smile; a regular guy but, hey, brilliant . . .

". . . as we attempt to reconcile our guest's mystical claims with metaphysical reality . . ."

The psychiatrist sitting behind Lynn and Bill Hill said, "He doesn't know what the fuck he's talking about."

Lynn was looking way up at the grid of lights and cables high against the studio ceiling, crisscrossed rows of at least a hundred lights to shine down on Howard Hart's little fake-library set in the corner of the studio.

Bill Hill said, "He doesn't know how to smile either. Look at him, he clenches his jaw and shows his teeth."

"As opposed to his natural shit-eating grin," Lynn said. "He's a honey."

"I'm told," Howard Hart was saying, "the boys at the network expect this evening the biggest audience response we've had since a son of a . . . famous singer"—pause, shit-eating grin—"walked off the show a few weeks ago." Pause, smile. "Now, if you've got questions for our guest, keep your phone handy and call them in. Or if you have comments to make, come on, let's hear from you. I guarantee our guest is going to be controversial, to say the least. I've put a dozen extra operators on duty just to handle your calls and I know, at least my regulars out there"—pause, smile—"won't let me down. So right now, let's bring on our guest."

The floor manager, wearing a headset, standing midway between the two Ampex cameras on the stage, turned to the audience clapping his hands. The audience picked it up, maintaining the applause as Juvenal came out from somewhere, took Howard's extended hand—Howard reaching across his giant desk—and sat down in a swivel chair that was a scooped plastic shell on a chrome base.

Bill Hill said, "Jesus, he looks like he just got out of the hospital."

"It's from the Center," Lynn said, "the clothes room."

The suit, a gray-striped seersucker, hung on him, lifeless, at least a size too large.

"I tried to get him to buy a new one. He likes it."

Howard Hart was leaning on his desk staring at Juvenal, letting the silence lengthen dramatically. Finally he said, "Your name is Charlie Lawson and you're sometimes referred to, affectionately I presume, as Juvie. Well, I'm going to be noncommittal this evening and call you Juvenal. How'll that be?"

"The only way he could be noncommittal," Lynn said, "is if you cut his tongue out." In a moment, staring at Juvenal, her mood changed and she said, "Awww, look at him. Isn't he neat?"

Howard Hart was saying, "What I'd like you to do first is explain your stigmata in your own words, exactly what it is, and then tell us how you do it. But first, this word from one of our sponsors."

Lynn said, "You see what he's doing? The first thing he says, for God's sake."

"Just take it easy," Bill Hill said.

"I don't do it," Juvenal said. "It just happens. I'd like to add that I don't say it's mystical, either, as opposed to your reference to metaphysical reality. What do you mean by that?"

"You believe in God," Howard said, ignoring the question.

"Yes."

"You believe in miracles."

Juvenal settled back, resigned. "Yes."

"You were a Franciscan, which is a particularly . . . mystic-orientated order, weren't you?"

"I was a Franciscan brother. I don't know how mystical they are."

"You believe God can work wonders, if He chooses, through you."

"If He wants to."

"Would you say you're quite impressionable . . . suggestable, perhaps naive?"

"I probably am," Juvenal said.

"So that your five so-called wounds are not a miraculous mystical representation of Jesus Christ's wounds, divinely given to you by God, but are very probably caused by your own psychic suggestion."

"It could be," Juvenal said.

"What do you do, squeeze your eyes closed, concentrate on a crucifix, and hold your mouth a certain way?"

"No, I don't do any of that."

"You pray? Say, come on, God, give it to me? Let's show 'em I'm a holy Joe, a living, breathing saint, a miracle-working mystic right out of the Middle Ages?" Howard Hart waited. "Well?"

"Would you repeat the question?"

(Lynn laughed.)

"Why do you think God would single you out for this . . . wondrous gift? What's so special about you?"

"I don't know that He does."

Howard Hart smiled at the camera. "Well, you're modest. Is that part of the image? Oh, my goodness gracious, why me, Lord? Let me ask you a question. Why'd you come on my show?"

Juvenal hesitated. "You invited me. I thought it might be a good opportunity . . . well, I thought, why should I hide? If I have this . . . it isn't something I'm ashamed of."

"Wait a minute," Howard said. "Hold it just a cotton-pickin' minute. *I* invited you? I seem to have the impression your manager came to *me*."

"He's not my manager."

"—and made a deal stating that you, a so-called servant of God, self-proclaimed instrument of His mercy, would not appear on this show for less than"—looking directly at the camera—"one million dollars."

Juvenal was sitting erect in his chair, holding onto the curved sides. "I'm supposed to be paid for this?"

"You didn't sign a contract?"

"I signed something, I don't know what it was."

"You didn't read it?"

"No. I glanced at it."

"So you're telling me you know nothing about receiving one . . . million . . . dollars? You want people to believe you're appearing here as a public service, an act of charity?" A laugh came out of Howard Hart's shit-eating grin. "We'll be right back after this message."

Lynn said, "You son of a bitch."

Bill Hill glanced around, putting his hand on her arm. "Take it easy, okay? How many times did I try to talk to you? You refused to hear anything about it, right?"

"You made a *deal?*"

"It's not anything like he's saying it is."

"How much?"

"He's using it, trying to make him look dumb, that's all."

"How *much?*"

"Guaranteed four hundred thousand," Bill Hill said. "Juvie signed the contract in Howard's office; I saw him looking at it."

"But you didn't tell him about the money," Lynn said. "You didn't say, 'You're getting four hundred thousand dollars.' Did you?"

"The amount isn't definite till we find out how many stations put it on. So . . . we get the check, I was gonna surprise him."

"We—" Lynn said.

"You're in on it."

"I don't *want* to be in on it." Very tense, biting off the words.

"I'll tell you the whole thing after. Have we had a chance to talk? You go away, you don't even tell me you're going."

"How much do you get out of it? Since it's his money."

"Well, I set it up and everything. I had to sell Howard."

"How much?"

"Half sound about right?"

"Tell me," Howard Hart said, "how much have you made so far as a professional stigmatic and miracle worker?"

"Nothing," Juvenal said.

"This'll be your first million then. What're you going to do with it?"

"I didn't know I was getting anything."

"Uh-huh," Howard said. "Well, now that you know, what'll you do with it? A million dollars. By the way, as a religious miracle worker, are you a tax-free entity?"

Juvenal was frowning a little, thoughtful, swinging very slowly from side to side on the swivel.

"I don't know what I am."

"Well, I'd say you're rich, for one thing. So what do you do with all your money . . . spend it on your girl friend? Which brings up an interesting facet . . . the miracle worker's what, lady friend? I'd like to know a little more about that side of your life—what do you call her, your mistress? The stigmata's inamorata?"

("Oh, my God," Lynn said.)

As Juvenal said, "Lynn?"

"Lynn Marie Faulkner, who, I believe, lives out in sin city, I mean Somerset Park."

("Jesus," Bill Hill said.)

("Rotten son of a bitch," Lynn said.)

"But first—let's save that," Howard said. "I don't want to get ahead of myself and open up too many cans of worms at once, uh?" Pause. "Off the record though, you aren't by any chance working on some kind of a religious sex manual, are you? I understand that's a lucrative new field."

(Lynn stood up.)

"But first—as I mentioned—I want to bring out someone whose appearance alone will give testimony to still another facet of your life-style and very mysterious, I might add, personality . . . right after this message."

Bill Hill said, "Where you going?"

Lynn didn't answer, she pushed past him to the aisle. Bill Hill thought she was leaving and got up to follow, thinking she was going to run out, emotionally unstrung or something, and he'd have to calm her down and try to get her back in.

But Lynn wasn't running out. God no—as Bill Hill stood watching—she was marching up on the stage past the cameras and the floor manager over to Howard Hart's fake-library set. Now Lynn was talking a mile a minute, Howard standing, trying to calm her down, and the floor manager was bringing over another swivel chair.

In a close-shot of Howard Hart, leaning comfortably on his desk, confiding straight out to his millions of viewers, he said, "Well, if you haven't come to expect the unexpected on 'Hartline' by now . . . we were speaking about a young lady by the name of Lynn Marie

Faulkner . . . well, speak of the devil''—grin—''and I
mean that figuratively, because here she is live, and I
might add, very much alive . . . Miss Faulkner.''

As the second camera was cut in, Howard Hart's
millions of viewers saw Lynn sitting right there next to
Juvenal in the same kind of chair, legs crossed—nice
legs—arms folded, jaw clenched? Maybe. The viewers
saw a good-looking girl who was doing everything she
could to remain in control and not go over the top of that
giant desk for Howard Hart's throat.

Great stuff. Howard had two rings going here, on his
library desk set. He rose, the camera following him, and
took his viewers over to the third ring at center stage, to
a figure encased in plaster lying on a narrow, mobile
hospital bed. Curtains served as a backdrop.

Howard said, "If Lynn Marie can hang on just a
minute, first I want to introduce somebody to you—"
Howard began turning a crank at the foot of the bed. As
he did, the head of the bed began to rise, bringing with
it . . .

"—Mr. August Murray," Howard said.

. . . lying on his back, presented to the camera and the
audience with his arms extended straight out to the sides,
August immobile in a body cast that reached from head
to hips, revealing only his face, peering out of an oval
opening, and his hands hanging limp from the ends of the
outstretched cast. A white plaster crucifix on a hospital
bed, August in there, somewhere.

"Mr. Murray," Howard said, "is, or I should say,
used to be, a good friend of Juvenal's. But it seems there
was a misunderstanding, for which Mr. Murray cannot be
held blameless, no. In fact, according to the Troy Police,
who arrested Mr. Murray and released him on a five-
thousand-dollar bond, he did intend to do great bodily
harm to one Lynn Marie Faulkner, sitting right over there.
That's how the charge against Mr. Murray is worded.

Also something about carrying a gun in the commission of a felony, which is a no-no and an automatic two years. Though I would say from looking at him the great bodily harm was performed on Mr. Murray. Would you agree with that, sir?'' Howard Hart, holding his mike, leaned in close to August.

"He says yes, he'd agree. Now, what happened was Juvenal, in protecting his . . . lady friend from Mr. Murray, who it seems was in a fit of temper, a little p.o.'ed, so to speak . . . *threw* Mr. Murray bodily off a second-story balcony. Now listen to this. Breaking *both* his arms . . . his collarbone . . . four ribs . . . and cracked a vertebra or two in Mr. Murray's neck. The doctors say he'll be in that body cast about five months, maybe longer, due to our miracle worker laying his hands on him. Hey, wait a minute. Which makes me wonder, hey, if I should have risked shaking hands with Juvenal when he came on. Man, oh, man. But seriously, I'd like to confront Juvenal with the question, does he have the same power to harm as he does to heal? And . . . we'll talk to Lynn, our miracle worker's special squeeze''— winking at her—"as soon as we come back.''

Lynn said, "Let's go.''
Juvenal was staring at August.
"Come on, let's get out of here.''
"It's too late,'' Juvenal said. "We're in it now.''
"Listen, people walk off his show all the time. You can see why.''
"He's amazing, isn't he?''
"*Amaz*ing? He's crucifying you.''
"You were right, he's a rotten guy; and he enjoys it. That's what's amazing.'' Juvenal's gaze moved to August. "There's a lot going on, huh?''
"God,'' Lynn said. When Juvenal got up she said, urgently, "Where you going?''

"I want to tell August something."

Howard Hart said, "Well, we're starting to get phone calls, and what all of you out there seem to want most is not a lot of claims, but to actually *see* Juvenal heal someone. As one fella said, 'Let's see his act.' Hey, I couldn't agree with you more. You say you can do something; prove it, let's see it happen. But the network boys, who're all lawyers at heart, said definitely no. You get an unfortunate cripple on the show who expects to be healed—what if it doesn't come off? I said, then we'll be exposing a fraud. But they said uh-unh, we'd be exposing ourselves to a lawsuit. So there you are. We *are* going to talk to people, however, who claim to have witnessed Juvenal's healing power." Howard paused, raising his gaze to the glare of lights. "There's a Father Nestor in the audience . . . Father Nestor, are you out there? . . . Father Nestor was also a missionary in Brazil and witnessed a number of the so-called miracles or spiritual healings. Father Nestor? . . . Well, we'll see if we can locate him. Meanwhile . . . I see Juvenal's over there chatting with Murray the mummy—Kenny, can we get a mike over there? No, I'll tell you what. First I'll talk to Miss Faulkner, who seems just a little bit edgy . . . What's wrong, Lynn? . . . and find out what it's like to shack—oops, just a slip—I mean *live with* a miracle-working stigmatic and prospective twentieth-century saint. Lynn? . . . What's it like?"

Lynn said, "You know what you are?"

"I'm a bleep," Howard said, "because if you say what I think you're going to say, that's the way it'll come out. But seriously, tell us about Juvenal. What's he like?"

"You're a rotten whoop-whoop," Lynn said to the millions of television viewers.

Howard looked up at the floor manager. "Kenny, are we using bleeps, whoops, or wipes?"

"On the five-second delay, whoops," Ken said.

Howard smiled at Lynn. "You were saying?"

She took her time, trying to adjust, relax.

"Go on, I'm not going to hurt you."

Quietly she said, "I saw him bleed. At least two hundred people saw it."

"I'm not questioning that," Howard said. "I accept the fact he has this bleeding act."

"It's not an act."

"All right, this phenomenon. But what I want to know about is your relationship. Are you living together?"

"No, we're not living together."

"But the two of you were away for a week. Did you sleep in the same room?"

Lynn was tense again. "What does our personal life have to do with it?"

"Honey, you walked on my show uninvited. If you choose to sit there, I can ask you anything I want. Do you and Juvenal sleep together?"

"I'm not gonna answer that."

"What do we do," Howard said, "all the viewers out there—just look at you? You come up here, you want to protect him—" Howard paused. He said then, gently, "Lynn, are you in love with the guy?"

She hesitated, suspicious, then nodded. "Yes, I am."

"Then what's wrong with talking about it? And he's in love with you?"

Still hesitant. "We love each other, yes."

"Hey, it's beautiful," Howard said. "You're young, you're in love. Heck, then what's wrong with sleeping together?" He paused. "Unless you're ashamed to admit it, feel it's something dirty, obscene." Howard frowned. "If you're in love, why would you feel guilty about sleeping together?"

"I *don't* feel guilty. I haven't said anything about

. . . our relationship.'' The son of a bitch, he was even worse than she thought.

"You haven't denied anything either. Hey, I'm not judging. If you're having an affair with him, that's your business—

"—but if you bring it on my show then it becomes *my* business because, honey, I can talk to you about anything I want—'' Juvenal heard Howard say, as he was trying to hear what August was telling him through his clenched teeth, painfully, with a great effort.

". . . kill you, ruin you and everything we work for. Get her off. Get rid of her. Tell him bring the microphone here. I'll tell him what I said, I don't blame you, even what you did. It isn't your fault. It's her.'' The effort of speaking made August close his eyes for a moment to rest.

Lynn was telling Howard Hart he didn't *talk* to people, he made speeches, fascinated by the sound of his own voice; he didn't misquote, as she had suspected, he quoted things that were never said; he implied things with a lot of shuck-and-jive innuendos.

Juvenal was looking at Howard's clenched-jaw smile on a TV monitor that was beyond the hospital bed, on the other side of the stage. Howard reminded him of August, who'd lie healing in his plaster shell for five months and then break out to become . . .

Juvenal leaned closer to the bed. "August?''

August opened his eyes.

"Listen, I'm very sorry it happened,'' Juvenal said. "But you're still full of shit.''

He returned to the library set as Howard was introducing another important message from a sponsor.

A girl walked up with a handful of notes, sheets of paper, and laid them on Howard's desk—off-camera now

to the millions of viewers watching a detergent salesman
getting a housewife to rip her husband's T-shirt in half.
Howard got busy with the notes, grinning as he looked
through them.

Lynn stared at him.

Juvenal said, "He's right. You can't appear on
something like this and hide."

Lynn didn't say anything. Juvenal looked over at
August and back to Lynn.

"What's your book say? You don't have to be mad or
upset unless you want to."

"Well, I want to," Lynn said.

"He makes it look like we're hiding something."

"You want me to tell him everything, get clinical?"

"I think you ought to use your words instead of his."

"And get whooped off the air?"

"What difference does it make?" Juvenal said. "Is it
that important?"

"Isn't it? What people think of you," Lynn said,
"God, the difference between what you're really like and
the way he makes you look?"

"That's what I mean," Juvenal said, "let's just be
ourselves."

"And come off looking like a couple of yo-yos."

He smiled at her. "It's the chance you take. But in the
light of eternity, who gives a shit?"

"I'll tell you something," Lynn said, "I really love
you."

"Will you do something for me?"

"Sure, what?"

"Go over and sign August's cast."

See how simple it was? Just be yourself.

Simple maybe, but not easy, listening to Howard Hart.

" 'How . . .' " Howard read with dramatic pauses,
" 'do you reconcile religion . . . the claim that God is

using this man as His instrument of mercy . . . with raw sex? The two are totally incompatible.' '' Howard lowered the sheet of paper to his desk. ''Well first, let me remind you, statements made on this program do not necessarily express the opinions of myself or the network. However in this instance I would ask the same question. . . . Lynn? How *do* you reconcile religion and sex?''

''I don't know what you're talking about,'' Lynn said, ''and I don't think you do, either.''

''Well, my viewers seem to feel—and I'm referring to the majority of calls we've been getting—that you and Juvenal are talking out of both sides of your mouth at the same time. He pretends one thing, but you prove the opposite.''

''What have I said?''

''Let me read another one. 'Mr. Hart . . . you approach dangerously close to sacrilege when you submit to us a man of God who openly admits consorting with an unmarried woman.' '' Howard looked at Lynn.

She said, ''What's the matter with being an unmarried woman?''

''Consorting with, I believe the caller said, a holy man, or a man of God.''

''Yes, we consort quite a bit,'' Lynn said. ''We're very big on consorting.''

Howard waved a note at her. ''A woman called to say she let her eleven-year-old daughter stay up to watch the show, but had to send her off to bed as soon as you began telling about your affair.''

''She could've switched to 'Starsky and Hutch,' '' Lynn said.

''Another one,'' Howard said. ''Listen to this. 'What's in his mind? What can he be thinking of? To bear the marks of Christ crucified and yet submit his flesh to lust. There is reference in the Bible to the Anti-Christ coming and appearing in the guise of the Lord. Could it be that this man is the direct opposite of what he says he is?' ''

"What do I say I am?" Juvenal said.

"It seems to me"—Howard leaned heavily on his desk, studying Juvenal—"in what I've been reading about you, you've not only implied but stated categorically you have some kind of a divine pipeline, God working through you in mysterious ways . . . that is, when you're not messing around with Miss Faulkner here. Would you say that's a fairly accurate appraisal of your claim? Some kind of a messiah?"

"I know what you are," Lynn said. "You're an opinionated little man with a dirty mind and a twenty-nine-dollar hairpiece and if this excuse for a show ever gets more than a ten share I'll kiss your whoop."

Howard grinned, because he loved it and couldn't be insulted or hurt. He said, holding up the handful of notes, "And how about all these people? We've gotten some two hundred calls already and the majority of them, by far, question your illicit relationship—"

"*Illicit?*" Lynn said.

Juvenal got up from his chair.

"Don't leave without saying good-bye," Howard said.

He wasn't leaving. One of the cameras followed Juvenal across the stage to August Murray's hospital bed.

Lynn and Howard Hart both watched him until Howard said, "Illicit . . . we'll get back to our miracle worker, he's going to check on his friend . . . yes, I call it illicit and it seems hundreds of others do too. An illicit conjugal affair made more promiscuous by the circumstances—"

August could not hear very well or turn to face the voices or get anyone's attention. He was nauseated and his eyes and nose itched. He was miserable. He told himself several times he wanted to die and remembered, in that moment just before he saw Juvenal's face in front of him, that tomorrow was the anniversary of the death of Saint Augustine and he knew something was going to happen to him.

Juvenal said, "August?"

"What?"

"August—"

"What!"

Staring at the face, the eyes, sorrowful eyes, as Juvenal leaned very close, as if to take him in his arms.

August felt strange. Like he was floating, dreaming. He saw Juvenal's face again, the eyes. He saw Juvenal's hands. He could see and feel the fingers—pressing his eyes downward—he could see the knuckles, fists. My God, he was here but his body had no feeling. There was no itching or nausea. There was a sound. The audience? The audience was standing up and sounds were coming from the audience. But the other sound was different and wasn't from people. It was close around him, part of him, and not from out there where everybody was standing, or from the camera with the red-dot light that was moving in toward him. My *God*—he could feel hands on his body. On his chest. On his ribs.

He could *hear*. He could *move*.

He could lower his arms and raise them and lower them. He could swing his legs off the hospital bed.

The body cast, the plaster crucifix, was gone.

25

They would talk with pauses, seeing it again.

Antoinette Baker said, "It was like red paint. You know it? It didn't even look real."

"It was real," Bill Hill said.

"I know it was real, but it didn't look real. That's what Richie said too, at the church. I want to call him, but— you think it's too late?"

"It was real. The way it was coming through his shirt?" Bill Hill said. "You notice that?"

"I mean it didn't look real on the plaster cast, on the white," Antoinette said. "How'd he do that? Take it off."

"How did he do it? He pulled it off. Took it by the neck part—I think that's what he did. You want another drink?"

"Are you kidding? There's our waitress, there."

"If he can do what he did—" Bill Hill said. He signaled the Perfect Blend waitress in her black outfit, holding up two fingers and nodding. "That part was different than at the church."

"It was the same thing," Antoinette said.

"But it was different because you could see it," Bill Hill said. If he can do what he did—I mean, Jesus, the man had two broken arms, a broken neck, broken ribs—

227

then he can pull off a cast. What difference does it make how? You know how a doctor does it, he uses an electric saw.''

"I had a fractured ankle once,'' Antoinette said. "I slipped and fell off the goddamn bar. Where some beer was spilled.''

"You believe it?'' Bill Hill said.

"What?'' Antoinette said. "Do I believe it? I saw it. Everybody did.''

"No, they didn't,'' Bill Hill said. "They were looking at it—I mean people watching TV—but I'll bet they didn't really *see* it. Even Howard Hart and he was right there.''

"That shitbird,'' Antoinette said. "He had to've seen it.''

"But you notice how he got the camera back on himself right away?''

"I was watching August. I thought he was gonna take off.''

August, waving his arms, turning his head, moving his arms up and down, flexing his wrists, standing in his Jockey shorts with the hospital pajama pants down around his ankles; then kicking them off. Jockey shorts, white socks, and sandals.

Howard Hart standing up and then sitting, standing again, waving to get a camera and yelling at Kenny, the floor manager, "*Kenny, get the fucking camera over here!*'' for millions of viewers to hear without a bleep, whoop, or a wipe.

"See, that part happened fast,'' Bill Hill said. "Even looking right at it—hey, what's going on?''

Howard Hart talking to a camera.

Juvenal standing there a moment, holding out his bloody hands. His coat open, blood showing on the front of his shirt.

Lynn going over to him.

Howard saying, "Come on and sit down. Tell us how you did it."

And Lynn saying, "Your ass, Howard." Still without a whoop or a bleep. "Take your show and eat it."

Lynn and Juvenal walking through the curtain backdrop. Gone.

But blood on the edge of the curtain.

Howard saying, "I did invite Mr. Murray, but without the least suspicion anything had been prearranged. Mr. Murray? Come sit down here. Tell us where you got the cast."

And August Murray saying, "My bones were broken, my body, look"—holding up his arms—"and now it's whole."

A subdued August walking off the set in his underwear and socks, streaks of blood on his face, on his body, as Howard Hart called after him. Howard sitting down then and saying to the camera, "How'd you like to follow an act like that?" Smiling.

Bill Hill said, "Something was different about him. You don't know him, but something was different. He was a different person."

"August?" Antoinette said. "I talked to him last week, here. He seemed different, I know what you mean. Other people wouldn't know it; but Christ, they saw him waving his broken arms, his *healed* arms."

"But they listened to Howard," Bill Hill said, "almost another hour. You heard it."

"I couldn't believe it," Antoinette said.

"That's what I'm saying, they were looking at it, all the TV viewers, but what did they see? What, we come to find out, made the biggest impression on them?"

For thirty-eight minutes, not counting commercials and station breaks, Howard Hart took selected phone-ins directly and chatted with members of his network audience. Some wondered, "What was *that* all about?"

And Howard would say, "You saw it. What do you think?" Reply: "I think they ought to work on their act." Or: "The cast was a good touch. What was it, open in back?" But the great majority of the callers, and the telegrams that came in, said things like:

"Where do you find them? Even better than your transvestite interview, a *saint* who's living in sin. Wow."

"You should have warned everybody you were going to have an X-rated show."

"Your language on the air is in extremely poor taste, unpardonable."

"Next thing you know we'll find out the pope has a girl friend."

"If that isn't sacrilege, the flaunting of sex by a so-called religious person, what is?"

"Her guilt was obvious. You could tell by the brazen way she showed her legs."

"To disguise promiscuous sex as love was the worst lie of all."

"Again your show condones and glorifies immorality."

"And he calls himself a messiah."

"The shocking fact is not that he's a fraud—he may be sincere—but that he has feet of clay."

"What can God be thinking?"

And so on.

Howard Hart saying to each of his callers, "Hey, it was nice talking at you."

The USBS network received, at final count, 273,484 letters, postcards, wires, and phone calls in regard to the Juvenal telecast, a record number of responses. Still, "Hartline's" Nielsen for that Saturday evening came in a poor fourth behind (1) the CBS Movie, *Shark's Treasure,* starring Cornel Wilde; (2) NFL Preseason Football, Detroit at Seattle; and (3) a rerun of "Starsky and Hutch."

Bill Hill read about it in the paper and said, "Jesus Christ."

August Murray read about it and said, "So be it."

Antoinette Baker read about it and said, "Wouldn't you know."

Lynn and Juvenal never did read about it. They drove out to L.A., stopping in Nashville and Luckenback, Texas.